Advance Praise for

"As a psychologist and a lover of mystery fiction, I recommend this book highly. The author knows how to amuse and entertain with her colorful descriptions of 'homo ludens'. However, under the fun and froth lurk wider issues which the author illuminates for us to measure our own inclinations and true nature. She does so with intelligence, wit and warmth. I suggest that a sunny summer book like this will nudge the world a bit closer to oneness."

--Jim McQuire
Counseling Psychologist, M.A.
San Francisco State University

"A most enjoyable and clever novel! I was fascinated learning about the geography and history that make Palm Beach the unique place it has grown into. This book will become a 'must' for visitors."

--Lady Walton
Writer, gardener,
widow of the composer Sir William Walton

A Fair Way
To Die

A MOLLY MILLER MYSTERY

A Fair Way To Die

It Happened in Palm Beach

Dagmar Lowe

Legacies Books
a division of Humanics Publishing Group
Lake Worth, Florida, USA

A FairWay To Die
© 2006 by Dagmar Lowe
A Legacies Books Publication
First Edition

Legacies Books is an imprint of and published by Humanics Publishing Group, a division of Brumby Holdings, Inc. Its trademark, consisting of the words "Legacies Books" and the portrayal of a sextant, is registered in the U.S. Patent and Trademark Office and in other countries.

Brumby Holdings, Inc.
12 S. Dixie Hwy, Ste. 203
Lake Worth, FL 33460
USA

Printed in the United States of America and the United Kingdom

ISBN (Paperback) 0-89334-421-4
ISBN (Hardcover) 0-89334-422-2

Library of Congress Control Number: 2005932126

This book is for my children, Virginia, Philip, Arabella and Lucinda with love and gratitude for their forbearance.

It is also in memory of two remarkable men: my father, H.B., and my first Palm Beach friend, C.A.

And of course for Harry.

All characters in this publication are fictitious. Any resemblance to real people, living or dead, is coincidental. I have taken artistic license with the location, the golf club and the workings of the police force/FBI for the sake of the story.

Dagmar Lowe

TABLE OF CONTENTS

List of Characters

Molly Miller, accidental sleuth

Emilio Gonzalez, Special Agent in Charge from the West Palm Beach office of the FBI

The *Residents* of Golfview Road (and houseguests):

The *Robertson* household:
Francis (Frank) Robertson, widower
Elizabeth Robertson, née Fellows, his late wife
Sam Robertson, their son
Sheila Wallace, their daughter
Bill Wallace, Sheila's husband
Willie, Bill and Sheila's son
Gillian Fellows, Elizabeth Robertson's brother
Morreen, Gillian's girlfriend
Marjorie Pitts, housekeeper
Maurice Dutroix, butler

Henry Standing, widower and friend of Molly's

Frederick Brownlow, single, President of the Evergreen Club

Osbert Harvey, bachelor, lives with his mother

Friends and Others:

Peggy and Martin Harris, friends of the Robertson family

Marylou Baker, gallery owner, friend of Sam Robertson's

Birdie Baker, Marylou's mother

Lucy de Silva, childhood friend of Molly's, visiting Palm Beach

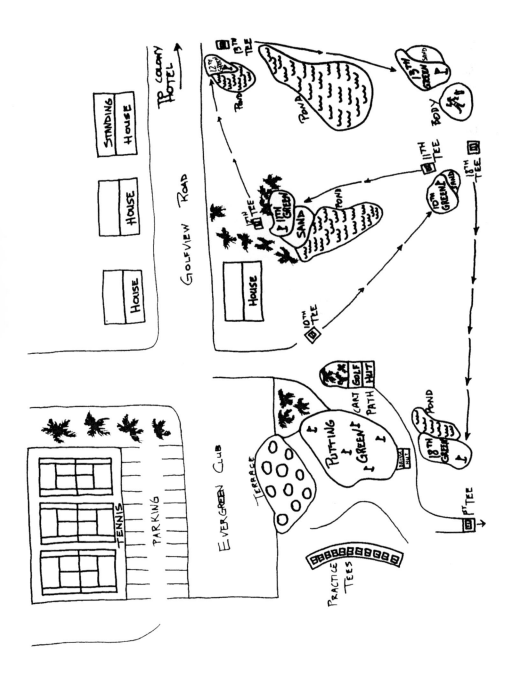

STANDING HOUSE

HOUSE

HOUSE

HOUSE

TO COLONY HOTEL

GOLFVIEW ROAD

13TH TEE

12TH GREEN

POND

POND

13TH GREEN SAND

BODY

11TH TEE

9TH TEE

11TH GREEN

SAND

POND

10TH GREEN SAND

18TH TEE

10TH TEE

GOLF HUT

CART PATH

PUTTING GREEN

STARTER HUT

18TH POND

18TH GREEN

9TH TEE

TERRACE

EVERGREEN CLUB

TENNIS

PARKING

PRACTICE TEES

3

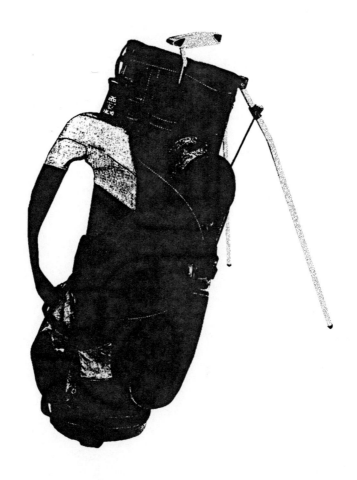

CHAPTER 1

FRIDAY

Osbert Harvey careened his golf cart back to the club house and came to a jolting halt, shouting for the caddies: "Help! George, Rick! Help! Jesus! Come quick! There's a dead body out there on the golf course, by the 10th hole!"

The words shattered the peace and quiet of the exclusive Evergreen Golf Club in Palm Beach, Florida at precisely 9:07 a.m. on a fine April morning.

Osbert had only set out for his game ten minutes earlier and was now back, looking flushed and uncharacteristically disheveled. Without waiting for details, George and Rick jumped into the nearest empty cart and shot off across the course aiming directly for the 10th hole.

Osbert Harvey, affectionately known to his many friends as, "Mr. Palm Beach", social arbiter of the club and the island as a whole, got out of his cart on unsteady legs. Even on the golf course he remained in character: urbane, elegant, affable. He removed his wide-brimmed straw hat and pulled a tangerine-colored silk kerchief out of the breast pocket of his well-cut linen jacket and dabbed his forehead. It was rare indeed to see this paragon of good breeding and manners so disturbed.

"I… I can't believe it… I had just finished the 10th hole…" he stammered, turning to the group of bystanders, club members and employees, who had gathered around him. "I was going to play the back nine holes, and when I looked over to the right, towards the 13th, I saw a golf bag lying on the ground, sort of abandoned, with nobody near it… So I went over and when I got out of the cart, I saw a body, half hidden in the bushes. It was a man… I couldn't see his face… but…" Osbert's voice trailed off.

There was a moment's silence. Then pandemonium broke out. The caddies came racing back, one of them speaking loudly and urgently into his cell phone. They jumped out of the cart and, running toward the pro shop, were met halfway by the manager who had already been informed that there was a problem. They whispered briefly before the manager turned to make a short announcement.

"Please, can you all move on?" he said, in a professionally calm voice. "There's been an accident. The police will be here any minute." Beckoning to Osbert, he said, "Mr. Harvey, will you please come to my office?"

Everyone was far too curious to disperse entirely. The club members moved back a few steps, reluctantly, towards the club house, watching the unfolding events. The caddies busied themselves with bags and carts.

Sirens were heard in the distance, coming closer, until they stopped in front of the club house. Officer John Fleming stepped smartly out of his police car. The manager came forward and was seen talking to him and pointing towards the golf course. Officer Fleming said a few words to the ambulance driver, got back into his squad car, followed by the manager, and both vehicles drove at great speed and against all laws governing the proper use of fairways, towards the body in the shrubs.

The day had started unremarkably enough. At 6:00 a.m. the hot Florida sun was already beating down, the streets were quiet and empty as usual. By seven o'clock, morning joggers panted along, clutching their water bottles. The first uniformed Hispanic maids dragged well-groomed pooches into the partial shade of the palm trees.

By 8:45 a.m. Palm Beach was wide awake. The lucky few who lived on this tiny island had finished their morning exercise. Breakfast had come and gone.

Palm Beach natives look after their bodies. They exercise —not too vigorously, but steadily—with long walks, swimming, a little yoga and gentle rounds of golf and tennis. It makes them feel better, sure, but their main motivation is to beat the biological clock—at which many are true champions. Everybody in Palm Beach looks ten to twenty years younger and, more importantly, lives ten years longer, than their counterparts in the grey cities of the North. They owe their longevity to the benign climate and a healthy life style, their looks mostly to the skill of cosmetic surgeons.

To maintain their youthful appearance Palm Beach residents eat and drink frugally. Iced water and tea beat champagne and whisky hands down. Charming restaurants serve mediocre, calorie-counted, low carb food at inflated prices. The social life is relentless but curtailed: even the most lavish parties start early with cocktails at 6:00 or 6:30 and end promptly at midnight, "Palm Beach midnight" that is. Elsewhere the clock shows only 10:30, but Palm Beach residents call it midnight and drift off to bed—to get ready for another hard day's play.

For all those not familiar with the island, it is somewhat surprising to discover that this well-known resort, some sixty miles north of Miami, is just a sliver of a sandbank, all of fourteen miles long and never more than half a mile wide. But its size is in reverse proportion to its economic-financial importance. The island boasts more billionaires per square mile than any other place. The Vanderbilts, Woolworths, Astors, Fords, and Dodges all have, or had residences here. It attracts big names in show business and the media (Rod Stewart, Jimmy Buffett, Rush Limbaugh) and rich and/or titled Europeans. The Churchills and Marlboroughs settled here, and the Duke of Windsor used to visit, as have other members of the British Royal family, especially on polo playing and fund-raising tours. Unemployed royalty, i.e., those deposed and in waiting, are particularly eager and welcome guests. There are a few, though not too many, artists and writers. Politically, Palm Beach achieved brief prominence when President Kennedy used his father's ocean front villa as unofficial winter White House (which necessitated the building of a presidential nuclear bunker on nearby Peanut Island).

This latter-day playground of the rich and famous was developed from a mosquito-infested, alligator-riddled, brushwood-covered swamp by the railroad magnate Henry Morrison Flagler in the 1880s, when he built his two stupendous hotels, the Royal Poinciana and the Breakers. What distinguished the island, however, and what even today is part of its special charm, was the cargo load of thousands of coconuts that had spilled from a shipwreck and covered the land with palm trees. But the place really came to life only after 1918, with the visit of two outstanding men: Paris Singer, heir to the sewing machine fortune and lover of Isadora Duncan, and the eccentric architect Addison Mizner.

They both arrived in bad health, ready to die. Instead, out of boredom, they started to do what they knew best: for one this was spending money, for the other, it was designing and building. Their first project was a convalescent home for officers of World War I. Singer bought Joe's Alligator Farm, and on this land Mizner erected an extraordinary building in an Arabic-Mediterranean fantasy style, surrounded by arcaded loggias, patios, fountains and tropical gardens. When war-wounded veterans failed to turn up, Singer changed its use from hospital to social club. It is now known as the Evergreen Club.

This was an entirely new style for Palm Beach residents who had, until then, lived in replicas of the clapboard cottages they knew from New England. The first to recover from this shock was Mrs. Edward Stotesbury, who had finally discovered a novel way of using her husband's money to catapult herself to the top of the social pyramid: Mizner had to build her a Shangri-la worthy of Queen Eva (as Mrs. S. was soon known). We don't know what Mr. S. thought about it all, but Addison Mizner was in seventh heaven. He had left a moderately successful builder's career in New York and California and could now design to his heart's content with virtually unlimited resources.

El Mirasol became the model for many of Mizner's later designs and those of his colleagues, notably Marion Sims Wyeth and Maurice Fatio. The vast thirty-six-room estate on the ocean was designed with gardens, tennis courts, pools, garages for forty cars and a private zoo. The interior boasted dramatic staircases, heavily coffered ceilings and doors, and tiled floors and walls.

This new and exciting, exotic and eclectic style found its pinnacle in the legendary Mar-a-Lago, a mansion with more than a hundred rooms on seventeen acres, stretching between the ocean and the lake, that Wyeth began and Joseph Urban finished for Marjorie Merriweather Post, the legendary breakfast cereal heiress. It continues its history as a show place for lavish parties, now as a country club owned by Donald Trump.

These heady days of building and entertaining on a grand scale lasted for only the best part of a decade. The depression, starting in 1929, decimated even substantial fortunes. Palm Beach residents down scaled and soon the white elephants of Mizner et al were culled. Sadly, only fourteen houses out of his oeuvre of forty have survived in recognizable condition.

After World War II another building boom started. Retired tycoons longed to display their wealth and erected large new houses, more manageable and restrained. Today however, owning an original Spanish-style Mizner villa is considered the finest prize of all.

In demographic terms the island is phenomenal. There are barely ten thousand year-round residents. During the Season (Christmas to Easter) this number swells to more than forty thousand with visitors, who are known as snow-birds, emigrating from the frozen East, New York, Boston, Toronto, and also Europe. The average age on the island has finally sunk from over seventy to late sixty. They may be old but, boy, are they rich. The Shiny Sheet, as the local Daily News is called, estimates that their readers are worth $11 Million—each. According to the Wall Street Journal, half of North America's corporate wealth is concentrated in Florida during the winter, and half of that belongs to the people who live in the candy-colored mansions along the Atlantic Ocean waterfront, on the east side of the island, or overlooking Lake Worth, as that strip of the Intracoastal Waterway is called, on the west side of the island.

Palm Beach Island is connected to its commercial counterpart on the mainland of West Palm Beach by three bridges, an easy ride by car or bicycle. As in politics, there is a fair amount of suspicion between East and West. Both communities have their own administration and mayor. The real barrier is a social one, a border more impenetrable than the Berlin Wall once was. Admittedly, the El Cid area of West Palm Beach has become fashionable, and other areas—Flamingo Park, Grandview Heights—are coming up in the world. Along the West Palm

Beach water front, increasingly luxurious condo buildings shoot up, at present ending with the astonishing twin towers of Palladio, but ultimately, only the Island itself provides the real social cachet—at a price.

Low cost housing does not exist in Palm Beach. "Regular" people live across the bridge on the "Continent". Until the eighties, all workers from the mainland were issued with a passport-like permit, with fingerprints, photograph and all. It just so happened that this was not enforced with white collar workers. Only when faced with a law suit were these regulations—deemed discriminatory and unconstitutional—revoked.

Politically and temperamentally Palm Beach is conservative, traditional and some would say reactionary. Class distinctions are sharp, but outwardly so subtle that the casual observer might not be aware of their existence. The two main religions, Judaism and Christianity, coexist peacefully, in general. There was, alas, a heated argument concerning the display of religious symbols, the crèche versus menorah war, but at last a truce was achieved.

On top of the social pyramid are members of old established families from across the country who migrated over the last hundred years to Southern Florida and took roots here, at least part time. The all-important Social Register of the top families exists here in the form of the Social Index Directory, published in Palm Beach, which lists all those who "have recognized social standing in their communities, both in Florida and their other residences". In the early part of the century, the original "Mr. Palm Beach", Charlie Munn (who had his mansion, Amado, built in 1919 by Mizner) compiled a very personal register: his annual Christmas card list included the names and private telephone numbers of all his friends, thereby defining the area's most select social group. This tradition is being continued these days by the Fanjul family, sugar barons from Cuba.

All those newly-arrived "nouveaux riches" (that you are rich to belong goes without saying) have to make an effort. It helps if you are well bred, gracious and generous to be admitted to the charmed inner circle of island life, especially if you manage to join one, or better two, of the prestigious clubs.

There are four important and expensive sports and social clubs on the island, of which the two most desirable are the Evergreen Club and the Bath and Tennis Club. It is probably fair to say that their members are almost exclusively WASPs. Admission is granted after a lengthy process of scrutinizing, vetting and checking. However, if the applicant, despite high caliber sponsors, is blackballed by only one member, he remains out in the cold, possibly forever.

The two other clubs are the Palm Beach Country Club (which has no WASPs) and Trump's Mar-a-Lago, where selection is widely influenced by financial considerations.

The joining fee can easily come up to a quarter of a million dollars plus considerable annual dues. Some smaller clubs, like the Beach Club and the Sailfish Club, attract a younger crowd because they are more affordable and inclusive. The Breakers Hotel has its own pricey club, popular for tennis and golf, but as it caters largely to their hotel guests, it is socially of little consequence.

Its suspicion of progress and modernity has stood the island overall in good stead. High rise-buildings are ruled out, as are chain stores and fast food outlets. Even Hamburger Heaven is so charming and inoffensive that the most ardent Luddites don't object. Preservation is preached and practiced, (alas too late for many historic mansions), and the island is all the more attractive for it. If this results in a certain sterility, an occasional unworldly touch of Disneyland, it is a cheap price to pay for defending a bastion of such beauty, peace, safety and tranquility.

On this fine April morning all was quiet as usual in Palm Beach. Expensive automobiles hummed discreetly along South Ocean Boulevard. The only jarring noise came from the leaf-blowers that burly brown Latin workers handled with gusto. Gardeners are forever trimming hedges, the crowning glory of the island (and no mean hurricane protection).

There is no place on earth where you find better, bigger, glossier, more pampered and manicured hedges. They grow 30 feet high and are coaxed into a wide variety of shapes, straight or rounded, meandering and undulating, lollipops and topiary. If hedges had not existed before, Palm Beach might have invented them. They have two important functions: they allow glimpses of half-hidden delights, thus hinting at their owners' taste, money and imagination, but at the same time provide much-valued privacy. This is important. Behind these verdant enclosures a lot goes on that escapes scrutiny, including murders, fraud and, some say, incest.

CHAPTER 2

Golfview Road is perhaps the prettiest street, certainly one of the most enviable addresses, on the whole island of Palm Beach. It is a short, private one-way street, running from west to east towards the beach, barely 500 meters long, situated parallel and just south of Worth Avenue, considered by some as the heart of the island. Cars can only enter by turning in from Worth Avenue at the Evergreen Club. It runs for one short block down to the intersection with South County Road past some of the most handsome mansions in Florida which face south, over-looking the golf course. The road continues, now called Hammon Avenue, past the Colony Hotel to South Ocean Boulevard and the beach.

Nearly all the houses on Golfview Road were designed by Marion Sims Wyeth and Maurice Fatio, contemporaries and friends of Addison Mizner's. The first one was commissioned by Marjorie Merriweather Post, after her marriage to Edward Hutton (uncle of the notorious Barbara) and before embarking on the creation of Mar-a-Lago. (The purchase price of the land was a very affordable one hundred dollars.) All of them are spacious, romantic, old world-looking stucco villas with swimming pools and often guest houses, even separate ball rooms, hidden in abundant exotic gardens.

Today, Golfview Road is one of the last bastions of Old Palm Beach. There are no young families. The only kids are those visiting their grandparents. The lucky owners are rich, quiet Americans. Among themselves they enjoy, if not intimacy, at least good neighborly relations.

No. 7 Golfview Road, a particularly grand villa in luscious gardens, was the home of Mr. Francis Robertson, known to his friends as "Frank", a widower who, at present, was visited by his two grown-up children, a son-in-law, a grand son, and his brother-in-law with girlfriend in tow. Life under his roof was comfortable, even luxurious, but conducted according to iron rules and a strictly observed time table: the day started with breakfast punctually at nine o'clock.

At 8:45 sharp Marjorie Pitts cast from afar a furtive, critical glance over the meticulously laid table. She was the housekeeper in this imposing buff-colored mansion. A two-story house in the Spanish style, it boasted a magnificent dining room, but its owner preferred to have breakfast served in the so-called garden room, a cool and lofty extension to the marble entrance hall, overlooking the patio from its row of French doors.

It was in this hall that Marjorie had taken up her spying position, half hidden behind a pillar. She was avoiding not the owner of the house, Frank Robertson, but the butler, Maurice Dutroix. Both had been in service here for almost a decade and their aversion to each other had heightened over the years. There had always been intense competition for supremacy, both claiming to be the one least dispensable to the smooth running of the household. Both wanted to be number one in the hierarchy of employees and in the esteem of their boss. Frank Robertson, well aware of this, was not averse to using the competition to his advantage. He was careful never to favor one of his two main minions without soon after rewarding the other.

This did nothing to create peace between Marjorie and Maurice, it rather resulted in a permanent state of truce, based on the realization that, although not satisfactory in every respect, their jobs were agreeable enough and so well-paid that it would be foolish to "rock the boat".

Marjorie Pitts was a handsome woman of indeterminate age. She would commit herself, should such indelicate questions ever arise, only to being "in her forties". She had been married once (so she said), had no children and was driven by the overriding obsession to "better herself", which in her book meant having a house of her own and being of independent means. Until such day, she fulfilled her duties in the Robertson household admirably. Efficiency, rather than charm, was her greatest asset. She tried to be pleasant and compliant in her work, but it did not come easily to her. She was tall and overly slim, thanks to a rigorous diet and exercise routine, and was always immaculately groomed. Her normally sober garments were occasionally interspersed with some incongruously girlish frock, often inspired by a magazine article advocating a total make over for the mature woman. She liked to wear outfits rather than dresses, preferably bought from Mildred Hoit on Sunrise Avenue. Today her agreeable but sharp features were unusually strained and there was an air of tightly suppressed tension about her.

The table in the garden room could seat eighteen comfortably, but today it was laid for only ten, in the usual style. Delicately embroidered white organza place mats rested on the massive oak table. The green and red Spode china echoed the trellis wallpaper. Two low silver vases were crammed with the pink, heavy-headed rosebuds so beloved in Palm Beach. On the sideboard waited jugs of orange juice, silver pots with coffee and tea and the chafing dishes that would soon be filled with eggs, bacon and sausages. Everything was spotless, nothing could be faulted.

Outwardly satisfied with her inspection, Marjorie could not suppress some small feeling of regret that perfection had been achieved by the butler whose responsibilities included the smooth serving of meals on immaculately laid tables. Thus was the definition and demarcation of their duties.

When Marjorie was first introduced to the household, some eight years earlier, she had tentatively strayed into the dining room, but had received an unconditional rebuff from Maurice, who had previously established his territory: mealtimes, drinks, attention to and care of silver, and the supervision of the outdoor staff were his domain. Added to that came the occasional demands made on him by his master, which in former times would have been handled by a valet: dealings with tailors, sorties to the dry cleaner, shoe repair and purchases of minor matters relating to Mr. Robertson's wardrobe.

Mrs. Pitts was left in charge of the kitchen and bedrooms, and the presentation of the reception rooms. The cook reported to her, as did the Spanish cleaner. She chose the menu, often together with her boss, and ordered the groceries, leaving the choice of alcoholic drinks and their purchase to the butler. Floral decorations fell into her department, as did replacements and additions to bed linen and towels, when necessary.

The ten places were laid for Mr. Robertson, his son Sam, his daughter Sheila and her husband Bill and their son Willie, who had all flown into West Palm Beach Airport the day before from Pennsylvania, and New York respectively. Two more guests had arrived the previous night on short notice, just a telephone call a few hours before. They were Gillian Fellows, the late Elizabeth Robertson's younger brother, and his girlfriend, a jolly, blowsy starlet, introduced only as Morreen. The occasion for this family get-together was Frank Robertson's birthday, the following day, which traditionally was celebrated in some style.

Three additional guests were also expected for breakfast: Marylou Baker, Sam's childhood friend, and Peggy and Martin Harris. Peggy had been the late Elizabeth's best friend and, childless themselves, she and Martin had always taken great interest in the Robertson children, and been on intimate terms with all the family.

The breakfast invitation had been a convenient compromise, relieving Frank of the need to invite Martin to a more important social occasion. Lately he had felt uncomfortable in his old chum Martin's company. He could not decide whether it was an unspoken reproach or a yet-to-come request that seemed to hang in the air every time the two men were alone together. There had been an intangible tension, and rather than confront it head on, Frank, at pains to avoid any potentially awkward tete-a-tete, had issued an invitation as expected, albeit only for breakfast, and thus social niceties were observed. The meal would be over in about an hour and could not possibly give occasion to private talk.

Francis Robertson embodied many virtues which were not always wholeheartedly admired by those nearest and dearest to him. One could mention an occasional lack of humor and a certain stiffness or formality in his behavior which was generally attributed to his early childhood spent in Germany. Those who had done business with him described his attitude as both suave and ruthless. If these traits were not always endearing, everyone agreed they were amply compensated for by his outstanding generosity and hospitality.

He was, and had always been, a stern father, and his relationship with his children was not particularly easy. He was fond of them, but not overtly affectionate. He had expected them to arrive for his birthday but was somewhat surprised by Gillian's appearance. After Elizabeth's death they had quarreled and consequently seen very little of each other in the intervening years. Gillian, however, had always been a conscientious uncle to Sam and Sheila and kept in touch with them.

The Robertsons' marriage had, by all accounts, been a happy one. Although so very different from his wife, Frank had loved and admired his wife's warmth and gaiety and she had valued his intellect and upright character. Under her influence, he had become softer and mellower and had even developed an interest in art. Elizabeth's father had left her a small collection of antique snuff bottles, and together, they had continued to add to this more valuable and unusual pieces.

This in turn had led Frank to look at Chinese porcelain. He liked what he saw, bought judiciously, and now some of his *famille rose* tureens were the envy of more than one museum. He got so involved in this new interest that he undertook several trips to China in his search for outstanding pieces to complete his collection. Although not unappreciative of beauty, for Frank this departure into the art world was also another way to accumulate wealth. He would never purchase an item for which he did not expect a handsome return. This was something that distinguished him sharply from a genuine art lover, who pursues an object of beauty and rarity regardless of material considerations.

Frank Robertson had always been a creature of habit. Since becoming a widower, this tendency had become even more pronounced and often gave rise in his friends to a smile and sometimes a snigger. A keen, but mediocre golfer ("I am strictly an iron man", he described himself) he embarked on a short round of golf every morning at eight o'clock, unless it rained heavily, which was rarely the case in Southern Florida. A

20

special, small bag containing a skeleton number of clubs waited for him in the hall and was returned there promptly before nine o'clock. As his house overlooked the Evergreen golf course, it took him less than five minutes before he teed off for the first hole, which was number ten. He followed with hole 11, then 12, 13, and completed his round with the 18th hole in exactly fifty minutes, before returning home for breakfast. He rejoiced every morning in the efficient beauty of this mini concourse that he had designed to his complete satisfaction. He had taken up the game rather late in life and would never be a champion, but playing regularly every morning had certainly improved his level.

Today as usual, Frank Robertson had turned up at the clubhouse just after eight, a familiar sight in his immaculate polo shirt (today it was a blue one) and the navy cap he habitually wore, with khaki trousers. His neighbors on Golfview Road joked that they could set the clock by Frank's appearance.

Of all his neighbors, and there were several high-minded personages of immaculate reputation, there was only one who could conceivably be considered a friend. This was Henry Standing, whose house was further down the road from Frank's, closer to the ocean.

Henry was a gentleman of independent means who, after having spent a lifetime reluctantly, but nonetheless successfully on Wall Street, had moved to Palm Beach permanently, where he retired to indulge in his diverse interests. Daily worries about bonds, derivatives and interest rates were replaced with fine tuning his golf and ballroom dancing skills. This joy had been severely curtailed by the premature death of his wife five years earlier.

However, it had to be said that life in Palm Beach for the born-again bachelor was an enviable one. The place was teeming with well-preserved, wealthy women, forever on the lookout for that rare commodity: a financially independent man, unencumbered by a wife or established mistress and still fit to walk unaided. Henry was a rather short man, and a little stout, with a tendency to put on weight. As the social life in Palm Beach revolved around food and drink (interspersed with exercise too gentle to counteract the intake of calories) his life was a constant battle to retain a midriff that could qualify as a waist. The women he "walked", however, maintained loyally that he was a handsome, trim man. (Slim would be too obviously a lie.) It was his bad fortune, he sometimes mused, that delicious food and fine wines gave him so much pleasure. A sweet tooth did not help either.

A lot could be gained, or in this instance rather lost, by a skillful tailor. Maus and Hoffman in Worth Avenue knew just how to cut a suit to draw attention to a gentleman's broad shoulders and disguise a protruding belly. Well-made clothes were part of Henry's pleasing appearance, as were bespoke shoes, lively bow ties and a discreet but unmistakable aftershave.

After a period of readjustment following his wife's passing away, Henry had returned to a happy life that, at least on a social level, left nothing to be desired. Rarely a day went by without an invitation to bridge, cocktails, lunch, dinner or a visit to the movies. Pleasant company could be procured with just one telephone call. The important thing to remember was not to get too close to any of his lady friends, but to spread his attentions evenly.

Henry loved his house, took pride in his garden, and got a kick out of his little foible, driving around Palm Beach in one of his two-seaters, all vintage convertible sports cars. "The girls" smiled indulgently and took action to protect their hairdos when invited into the passenger seat. Life was so perfect that even the occasional remembrance of his wife's death, of whom he was genuinely fond, cast no more than a slight, fleeting shadow over his contentment.

Today as every day at 8:35 a.m., Henry stood in his dressing room on the second floor of his pink villa overlooking the golf course. He had given up the game a few years before, after recurring problems with his back, but he greatly enjoyed watching other players. There, as expected, he spotted Frank Robertson approach the tee of the 13th hole. It was a long fairway, par four, and dangerously close to water on one side. Approvingly, he noticed that the ball rose high and flew a long way towards the green. An obviously satisfied Frank turned around, gave him a cheery wave and marched off to join his ball.

Henry completed his shaving and tried to remember which lady friend he was taking out for lunch that day.

* * *

Back at No. 7 the household showed acute signs of pre-breakfast activity. The butler sharpened his ear for the telltale sound of doors shutting and cars coming to stop on the gravel drive. He readjusted the napkins on the table, while appreciatively taking in a discrete whiff of bacon floating in from the kitchen where the cook assembled the dishes. Maurice Dutroix was a slightly-built man of medium height with carefully arranged thinning hair. As could be expected, he was always immaculately turned out in a dark suit and silver tie. Even on his days off he wore nothing more casual than well-pressed trousers and a long-sleeved shirt with just one top button undone, as a concession to tropical temperatures. He had a smooth, somewhat expressionless face that bore for work purposes a bland, noncommittal smile. His English was tainted with only a faint hint of a French accent which he was determined not to lose. He was aware that his nationality increased his professional stock. He was not married and lived quietly in a self-contained apartment above the garage block, as did the housekeeper. Maurice Dutroix seemed to have few friends, at least he was rarely seen socializing in Palm Beach. Marjorie Pitts was of course prejudiced, but she had not been too far off the mark when she once described her competitor and colleague as a man with "efficiency oozing through like an oil slick". As for his private life, she was not the only one to think of him as a "dark horse".

Upstairs the family finally stirred.

Sam Robertson, Frank's only son, was afflicted with the usual malaise suffered by weak sons of overbearing fathers: total subjugation. This was made almost inevitable by Sam's nature: he was an amiable second-born child, a gentle little boy, close to his mother and not given much to arguments and strife. It was ironic that due to his father's bullying and pressure, he had followed the prescribed career path into the law, where everything revolved around dispute and conflict. Instead of devoting his professional life to the arts, as had once been his dearest wish, he had become a junior partner in his father's old law firm in Manhattan. Sam looked much younger than his thirty-four years, almost boyish, with his soft blond hair flopping over his forehead. He knew his father would send him for a haircut at the Evergreen Barber Shop on Coconut Row before the day was out.

To say that he was unhappy would be an exaggeration. As he was more than sufficiently intelligent, the work posed no intellectual problems, indeed some legal puzzles genuinely intrigued him. His spare time was taken up with a small circle of friends, weekend visits to galleries and some modest collecting of contemporary art. His life in New York was easy, uncomplicated and, frankly, boring. In all these years he had never met a girl that could compete with Marylou Baker. He admired her, her knowledge, strength and determination, and adored her company. The prospect of seeing her in a few minutes excited him. Whenever he came back to Southern Florida, he blossomed under the strong sun. The heat did not affect him, he tanned easily and savored greedily the strong colors, the smells and sounds of the tropics. If only he could live here, now and forever, and paint. But that was out of the question. His father would harangue him until life was unendurable. Maybe one day, after early retirement or when his father was dead, he could come back.

At the moment he was thrilled to be home, in his old room, his very own bed, surrounded by the accouterments of his childhood: his tennis rackets and surfboard, family photographs and poetry books. His clothes were all laid out. He would shave later, so he could spend five more minutes in bed and dream.

Next door was his sister's room, today just as when they were children. All the second floor bedrooms had shuttered windows overlooking the front garden. They were reached on the other side from an open corridor that served as a verandah and led down the stairs to the hall. This way the rooms were cooled by cross-ventilation, and it made them, together with overhead fans, bearable even without air-conditioning.

Sheila was a delicate-looking woman in her late thirties, with her brother's fine features and his soft, pale coloring. When she made an effort, she could look very pretty indeed. Today, however, she paced the room with lank hair, her face drawn and devoid of any make-up, with an expression of anxiety that seemed to have become habitual. The unflattering white cotton dress she wore gave her a washed out appearance.

When she caught sight of herself in the mirror, she sighed. Oh dear, what had become of her? She still remembered the time when she had spent happy, carefree days in this house, with no other worries than to make a decision about where to play tennis and who to meet for cocktails. She had been an attractive young girl, the snappy little Lilly Pulitzer dresses in sugary pink and green and yellow citrus colors had suited her, they showed off her elegant legs and brown arms. After her marriage to Bill, she had changed her style to blend in with the more soberly-dressed citizens of Pittsburgh. First went the colors. Then, after Willie was born, she turned for convenience to comfortable trousers and practical tops. What is the point in dressing up, she said to herself, we hardly ever go out, Willie is never at home, Bill does not look at me and as for the money... he seems to regret every penny he gives me. Comparing herself to other, invariably more attractive women, in her opinion, made her feel woefully inadequate.

She saw less and less of Bill. Where did he spend his time? With his buddies? Or maybe he was seeing another woman? When had it all started to go wrong?

Bill Wallace had been the sporting hero at their college in Virginia. Charming, handsome, tall, he was much sought after by all the girls, but to her utter amazement he singled her out as his girlfriend. She had responded enthusiastically and to this day was convinced that her feelings for him had always been much stronger than his for her. After graduating he had proposed and a year later they were married. When Willie was born, seventeen years earlier, her happiness had been complete and he seemed pleased too. They were both disappointed that they could not have any more children, but at least they had Willie, on whom they doted.

Bill had a steady, if unremarkable, career in banking and appreciated that Sheila chose not to work. Being a wife and mother fulfilled her... at least until cracks in her marriage had started to show a few years ago. When she tried to talk to him, he was evasive, either too tired or busy with other matters. Willie, as if in response to his father's apparent indifference, had become moody and uncommunicative as well.

If only they had more money! Many times Sheila had been tempted to ask her father for help, but she knew that Bill would never forgive her for what he would see as disloyalty. Besides, she found it almost impossible to overcome her shyness and, yes, shame. Her father had been less than overjoyed with Bill as a son-in-law, and she was reluctant to give him grounds for triumph. Tears welled up in her eyes when she thought about her life and her marriage. All their laughter and tenderness had turned to Prozac and angst.

Where was Bill now? An hour ago, when he thought she was still asleep, he had stolen out of bed, dressed in the bathroom and had quietly left their room.

In the main guest room at the end of the second floor were Gillian and Morreen. Today this place bore testimony to man's never ending capacity to create chaos out of order.

The whole suite had a toile-de-jouy print theme in pale blue: the twin beds were swathed in it, headboards, bed skirts and duvets, the curtains, blinds and armchairs, all were covered with this charming French linen. Rugs, cushions, towels, lampshades, and even the waste paper basket, showed coordinated patterns in the same hue. What only a few hours ago had been a serene and elegant room, was now a wreck. Pillows and blankets had been discarded, suitcases erupted and their contents strewn over tables and chairs and on the floor. A dresser was piled high with papers, with a lap top computer precariously balanced on top. The dressing table was buried under an avalanche of cosmetics, pills and pots, potions and lotions, candles and combs, cheap jewelry, scents, scarves, hats, bags and bandannas. All that clutter was punctuated by screwed up paper tissues and the whole lot sprinkled with spilled face powder.

Gil pulled a face as he took in the surrounding mess. He had woken early after a restless night. He wanted to get up and out, there was something he had to do. While he was still thinking of an excuse to leave their bedroom at this hour, he saw to his relief, that Morreen had already made her own plans. Under half closed eyes he watched her, as she slipped into a flaming red kaftan and sandals. She piled her long hair loosely up on her head, secured it with some pins and finally added a large fake flower. She wound a mass of silver chains around her neck and arms and sprayed herself liberally with a musky scent.

Looking into the mirror she flashed herself a smile, made gigantic with Raspberry-Ripple lip liner. At last, after rummaging on her dressing table, she found some incense sticks and matches and picked them up. Morreen was heading for her meditation exercise in the garden.

She was a sweet girl, funny and quirky, pretty and not a bad actress, but his passion for her had cooled. She was just too young and, apart from a good sex life, they did not share the same wave length. The twenty-odd year time difference had become more and more noticeable, for him more than for her. Sometimes it seemed they inhabited different planets. Her eyes glazed over when he talked at length about John Huston (even his daughter Anjelica jutted barely into her youthful orbit), about Steinbeck, Kennedy, Maria Callas, even Grace Kelly. These names meant almost nothing to her. They had died before she was born and Morreen's passion was for living, NOW. The people who fascinated her—Madonna, Brad Pitt, the cast of "Friends"—bored him and so did her relentless obsession with the latest fad: Buddhism, meditation, macrobiotic diets, to name but a few.

His feelings for her had become more and more those of a bemused, older friend. She was kind and honest, but impervious to irony and took unimportant things frightfully seriously, as only the very young do. He still enjoyed her company, in limited amounts, and that was the reason why he had given in to her pleading to take her to Palm Beach. God knew what she expected to find here: Mr. Moneybags? The almighty producer? A British lord? Or was there some other reason that he did not know about?

He wished her well and would not like to lose her altogether but, frankly, he saw no future for them as a couple. Soon she might want some commitment from him and that he was unable to give her. It was time to move on, for both of them. These few days in Florida, he had decided, were by way of a sweetener, a farewell present.

Maybe it was time to go to work again. Luckily, or unluckily, this was for Gillian not a necessity, but an option. His father, a professor of English at Carlton College in Northfield, Minnesota, had left him and his sister enough money to get by. Elizabeth, ten years his senior, had settled early and married well. Gillian was more of a drifter, clever but without focus. A nine-to-five job was out of the question, but luckily he had always had a way with words and he loved books. Hence he had pursued a career as a freelance writer, first in journalism and lately as a novelist. He was never short of girlfriends, but so far, he had avoided matrimony. In New York he had been every hostess' dream of a spare man: a nice looking, well spoken, middle-aged bachelor, not poor and not gay.

To escape the social scene he had moved a year ago to a friend's guest cottage at Amagansett on Long Island. This self imposed exile was supposed to have concentrated his mind sufficiently for a serious onslaught on his magnum opus: The Great American Novel. So far he had spent years on research, jotting down the odd sketch and dialogue. Now, he had decided, it was time to put bum to seat and pen to paper. But fate had intervened. He remembered with a smile how he had met Morreen.

After two months of rigorous isolation, when he thought he would go mad without any more human contact than his biweekly visit to the grocer and the post office, he had decided one evening, on the spur of the moment, to go to a reading by a recently much talked about author, organized by Bookhampton in Easthampton. Predictably, the gathering had been dominated by earnest, bespectacled pseudointellectuals and he had soon gotten bored. He was just preparing to leave when a young woman chatted him up. She was sufficiently pretty to arouse his interest, and a few minutes later, they sat huddled in a corner, swapping their life and career stories. Morreen confessed that she was an actress, on her way to Hollywood, of course. So far she had been busy trying for small stage parts on, or even off, Broadway. When he introduced himself as a writer, she showed immediate interest.

"What did you say your name is?" He told her.

"THE Julian Fellowes?" she asked breathlessly.

"THE Gillian Fellows," he answered with a grin, not too clearly articulating, knowing what would come next. He just could not resist the temptation to carry on the misunderstanding a little longer.

"I LOVED Gosford Park," Morreen gushed.

"So did I."

"Are you writing anything at the moment?" she wanted to know. She was clearly thrilled to be in the company of a real life Hollywood celebrity.

"Sure. Writing isn't the problem. Publishing is."

"You've gotta be kidding... But hey, you sound American. I thought you were from England."

Ah, thought Gil, she is not dumb, just a little slow and he smiled.

"The Julian Fellowes you mean is English. I am Gillian Fellows, different spelling, different name, different man." He laughed when he saw her face. "I am a writer too, as it happens. Not quite so successful—yet."

If Morreen was disappointed, she managed to conceal it well under a pretty smile, and she began to show polite interest in Gil's work. After all, he was a writer, published even, and not unattractive. Half an hour later he had her telephone number and invited her to lunch for the following day.

He had remembered, just in time, that one of his best friends from New York was giving one of her famous lunch parties that day. He had kept the invitation, without answering it or intending to go, and now this seemed a heaven-sent opportunity to impress Morreen and at the same time check her out. He wanted to see how she handled herself in a fairly sophisticated social setting.

His friend Jordan Emery was a former model and, in her late sixties, still staggeringly beautiful and elegant. She was also smart and funny, and genuinely fond of her husband Tom, a business genius with a certain untamed charisma and an unpredictable temperament. He could be—but only with other people—somewhat self-centered and at times insensitive. With skill and patience Jordan always managed to smooth his easily ruffled feathers, soften his rough edges and pacify anybody Tom had irritated or offended. She flattered him, encouraged him, consoled him and in return for this loyal devotion, Tom worshiped the ground "Lovey" walked on. Jordan organized their vigorous social life in various homes with efficiency, style and unrelenting good humor—thanks to an iron constitution and self discipline that she had had ample opportunity to hone in her first marriage to an Italian count.

Tom's considerable fortune afforded them an enviable life style. They had the means and leisure to pursue all the things they enjoyed—traveling, entertaining, gourmet food, good paintings. Both of them were addicted to golf, Jordan mostly to please her husband. When they met, ten years ago, Tom was in the process of transferring all the passion that had subsumed his professional life onto the golf course. Achieving a "birdie" gave him, in those days, the same thrilling adrenaline rush that formerly only a successful merger had produced. Tom possessed all the characteristics of the typical Alpha personality, who had to excel at everything and was even compelled to beat his grandchildren at croquet. He could not help it: if he did not come first he would not play the game. When Jordan gave him a ping pong table, she made a fatal error. She won two matches against Tom—whereupon he packed up the table, never to play again.

His first wife, by whom he had two surprisingly well-adjusted children, had finally given up on him after thirty years of marriage, during which he had become phenomenally successful and she a nervous wreck.

In stepped Jordan, freshly and amicably divorced from the *conte*. She was a woman who just instinctively knew how to make a marriage—any marriage—work. When Federico had tried to conquer the world of theater—as producer, director, actor, whatever—she had cleverly cultivated the right circles in New York. When he had decided to return—temporarily as it turned out—to the land of his ancestry, she had found and renovated a suitably grand, crumbling palazzo in Rome while taking Italian lessons. If theirs had been, for her, never the most fulfilling relationship, she was the first to concede, however, that she was never unhappy with him and when asked why she eventually divorced him, she could only claim boredom. "I just could not bear to adjust his goddam' tie one more time."

After the languid count, Tom's nervous energy was an exciting change for Jordan and, once again, she knew exactly how to treat him. For such a glamorous woman, she was surprisingly solicitous and caring. Tom took himself exceedingly seriously and expected nothing less from those around him. Jordan supported him in this, as in everything. She shared his right wing political views and his anxiety about his health. A slight cold brought forth her concentrated concern for his physical well being. Trips to countries further afield than Canada—"everybody knows how germ-, virus - and bug-ridden the whole of Asia (or Russia, Africa, South America) is"—were undertaken in the company of a private doctor. It was this caring, warm, almost motherly attitude that set her above all the many other beautiful women around them and made her indispensable to Tom.

Every year they took the same sprawling old shingled house on Georgica Pond in the Hamptons for three months. For the rent they paid, they could have bought a small house in less salubrious parts, but it was this mansion they wanted. It was plain but handsome, had a dozen bedrooms, a pool and tennis court in its vast grounds. During these summer months, members of their widespread and extended families came to visit for a few days or weeks and could all be accommodated comfortably.

To keep house guests amused and Tom happy, Jordan entertained with imagination and panache. Twice a week, people flocked to her barbecues, cocktail parties, sit-down dinners and dances.

Invitations to the Emerys' house were coveted. Because they had so many real friends, they did not need to fill their rooms with the freeloaders that flock together wherever some peanuts and a warm glass of white wine are offered. Their parties were always a hit, thanks to Tom's money, Jordan's flair, and the help of an excellent Italian chef they imported every year from New York.

Gil, being the eligible bachelor he was, ranked high on Jordan's guest list, in New York as well as on Long Island. It took only an apologetic phone call from him to reaffirm his invitation and even have Morreen included.

The party, a casual buffet lunch, was already in full swing when they arrived. Morreen had been fashionably late when he collected her. Parking his car under the sprawling trees in the front yard, Gil could hear laughter and music. They were warmly welcomed in this circle, as were all newcomers, provided they had some decorative and amusement value. The dress code was casual, with the men in cotton slacks, even shorts, and the women in colorful resort wear, i.e., simple shift dresses or trousers and matching tops plus becoming straw hats. Most people knew each other: they all followed the well-trodden path of the leisured classes with metropolitan life in London or New York, summers on Long Island and the South of France, winters in Florida and the Bahamas, or skiing in Aspen and Gstaad.

To Gil's pleasure and surprise, Morreen conducted herself impeccably. She complimented her hostess sufficiently without gushing. She was charming with the mostly middle aged or elderly men, but not flirtatious, and although she looked different in the bohemian style she favored—flowing, layered gypsy skirt and lacy white blouse—she was pretty, fresh and unpretentious.

She even scored a hat trick by recognizing the guest of honor, the incomparably beautiful Dina Merrill, daughter of cereal heiress Marjorie Merriweather Post and Ed Hutton. Morreen showed a well-received interest in the older woman's exciting life: growing up at Mar-a-Lago in Palm Beach, three marriages and her distinguished acting career.

When they said good bye, Jordan gave her an affectionate kiss and demanded of Gil to come back with his charming companion another time, soon.

He happily obliged and from that day on his book moved further and further into the background, while his social life took over again. Once he and Morreen became lovers, they were inseparable for these blissful summer weeks. Golf at the Maidstone Club, by kind invitation of Tom and Jordan, was alternated by trips to Fire Island and Shelter Island, beach picnics, sailing, tennis parties, visiting galleries, wining, dining and dancing.

Those were their happiest days. At the end of the summer, Morreen had to return to New York, where her agent had lined up some auditions, while Gil tried to take up his work again.

Occasional weekend visits had kept their passion alive, eventually simmering down, at least for him, to a light hearted, uncomplicated romance that provided satisfactory sex, but hindered real progress with his work. That would now all change. He must send Morreen back to New York in a few days. Maybe he could stay here in Palm Beach for a while to write… and he had other plans. It would be nice to be with Sheila and Sam and, who knew, perhaps he could take up a certain thread that he had too easily let slip.

Gil shook himself out of his reverie, jumped out of bed and dressed in his running gear. He was not going to tell anybody where he was heading. Better to pretend that he was just going for an early morning jog.

CHAPTER 3

At 8:45 a.m., Marylou Baker sat on a bench in the small public garden on South County Road opposite the post office. Next to her leaned her old black bicycle with its big basket in front, containing a voluminous carry all. Bicycling was, for Marylou, both a pleasure and a main mode of transport. She lived in the Ocean Towers, an older apartment building overlooking the Atlantic, just north of the Breakers, and although she had a car, she used it mainly for trips out of town and ran all her errands on the island on two wheels only. It took her less than ten minutes to get to her job off Worth Avenue, a ride she enjoyed to the fullest every day.

There were three possible routes she could take with her bike from the "near North" of Palm Beach to the center of town, and this choice was usually her first decision of the day.

The most dramatic ride was the easterly one, past the Breakers golf course and the church, Bethesda-by-the Sea, then turning left towards the majestic pillar-fronted mansion of the Estée Lauder family, along South Ocean Boulevard and onto Worth Avenue.

Her most direct way led all the way straight down County Road, past the Town Hall, the police station and the fire house.

Most romantic was her favorite trip on the bike path, along the lake. This way she passed historic ground—if you can apply this term to a place just over a hundred years old. If this was her choice, she usually headed straight down Sunrise Avenue to Bradley Place, between the North Bridge and Royal Poinciana Way, a row of shops and three delightful restaurants, all with outside seating—ideal to see and be seen. Testa's and Chuck and Harold's were forever popular. Cucina had excellent Italian cuisine, and its bar was a great magnet for younger people on weekends.

From here, Marylou bicycled past the Royal Poinciana Plaza, a pleasing group of commercial buildings designed by John Volk in the classical Regency style. The most southerly of them, appropriately enough called the Slat House, was crowned by the only remainder of the Royal Poinciana Hotel after the hurricane of 1928: the little cupola of the original greenhouse.

Marylou could never pass here without remembering one of the most potent scandals to hit Palm Beach that had started here. On Saturday night, March 30, 1991, William Kennedy Smith, nephew of the late President, had met a young woman, Patricia Bowman, at a nightclub, Au Bar (on the site of the present Palm Beach Grill). Much later they had driven to La Guerida, the Kennedy mansion at 1095 North Ocean Boulevard. What happened next remained unclear, as the only people then present gave different accounts. The next morning Bowman went to the police and accused Smith of rape. The case came to court and after much legal wrangling—and huge public interest—the jury announced their verdict on the 11th of December: Smith was not guilty. A fair decision said some; a miscarriage of justice, influenced by the massive pressure of the Kennedy clan, said others.

After the Plaza, with its gorgeous, huge ficus tree on the south side, Marylou passed a very large white apartment block in horseshoe shape: the Palm Beach Towers. Here Flagler's Royal Poinciana Hotel had once stood (you are beginning to recognize the name?), then regarded as one of the wonders of the world. Building started in 1893, and it eventually grew into a six-story colossus, the largest wooden structure ever built in those days, with three miles of corridors. For $50 a day each, the 1,750 guests were looked after by almost the same number of employees, including one waiter for every four guests. For ultimate convenience Flagler had his and all private trains stop right outside the hotel.

In these days "Afromobiles" were the favored transport on the island: wicker carts, similar to rickshaws, pedaled by black laborers, carried visitors around. A special shuttle service, costing a nickel, ran between the Royal Poinciana and the Breakers, Flagler's second Palm Beach hotel (first called the Palm Beach Inn). This was a Florida East Coast rail carriage drawn by a mule.

The Palm Beach Towers was the scene of another scandalous event, also involving prominent Americans. Constructed in 1957 as a hotel, it was now a grandiose, luxurious apartment building, right on the lake (or Intracoastal Waterway) and with a spectacular pool area. In 1973, the newly married Helmsleys, Harry and Leona, (who later famously proclaimed: "Only little people pay taxes") arrived to spend the Thanksgiving weekend in their penthouse suite. (Actually they owned the building.) At 1:00 a.m., an emergency call reached the police from the Palm Beach Towers: A couple in penthouse suite A 514 had been viciously assaulted by an intruder and were rushed to the hospital. The man had been stabbed in the arm and the woman had suffered serious chest wounds. The victims were Harry and Leona. They claimed to have seen the attacker, a black woman—wearing a World War I gas mask! No suspects were ever found, so there was no case. Rumors persist to this day in Palm Beach that during a violent row Harry had stabbed Leona who, ever since, had a hold over him.

The Helmsleys did not go to court, until thirteen years later, when they themselves were charged with a criminal offence—tax evasion—and duly convicted. Harry was let off the hook due to his age and failing health, but the monstrously ruthless Leona did time inside.

After passing the Towers, Marylou steered down to the lake trail at the Flagler Museum, once the railroad tycoon's magnificent winter home. He built the white marble palace for his third wife, Mary Lily, whom he married in August 1901, just days after his divorce from wife number two, Ida Alice, who had been the first Mrs. Flagler's nurse.

Within weeks of their wedding, in 1883, Ida Alice had shown signs of being unbalanced. It started off with enormous spending sprees—costly even for her billionaire husband. Next she discovered that the late Russian tsar was the love of her life, with whom she kept in constant touch through the medium of the Ouija board. When she threatened to kill her husband, he had no choice but to institutionalize her. Secluded on their Long Island estate, aptly named "Satan's Toe", Ida Alice survived the longest: until 1930.

Flagler, desperate to marry the relatively young Mary Lily used his clout to achieve the near impossible: a divorce. In New York, where he lived, divorce was outlawed. Flagler, to achieve his goal, first moved to Florida, and secondly used his money and influence to change the law. Insanity was introduced as a ground for divorce (apart from adultery)—and Flagler made speedily use of it before it was renounced again shortly thereafter.

Mary Lily became the third Mrs. Flagler and her wedding presents were fit for a queen: a one million dollar check, two million dollars in government bonds, a string of graduated pearls of matchless beauty worth another million dollars (Mary Lily wears them in her portrait that hangs in Whitehall) and their new Palm Beach marble palace.

They entertained royally for just seven winter weeks of the year. Mary Lily loved music and dancing and their annual ball on Washington's birthday was legendary. Alas, they spent only ten seasons there before Henry Flagler died, at age eighty three. On March 15, 1913, Flagler was found unconscious on the marble floor of his bathroom and died five days later. His widow, thirty-six years his junior, survived him by just four years. She married again, but died childless, and the house was left to her family until it was sold as a hotel. In 1959 Jean Flagler Matthews bought the mansion and acquired as much as possible of the original furnishings. Whitehall was painstakingly restored and opened to the public as a museum, also used for functions and even the occasional ball, reminiscent of the sump-tuous parties held there a hundred years before.

Next Marylou, still on her bike, passed a church, called — no prize for guessing this one — the Royal Poinciana Chapel, built originally for Flagler's hotel guests. The charming old clap-board cottage next to it was Flagler's first home on the island, built in 1886 as the finest home in Southern Florida. He pur-chased it with forty acres of land and moved it closer to the lake, when he started building the hotel. After Flagler's death, the somewhat restless Croton Cottage, as it was then called, was moved to the ocean and suitably renamed Seagull Cottage. When in danger of being demolished, in the nineteen eighties, then mayor Earl E.T. Smith and the Preservation Foundation came to the rescue and found a final resting place (so far) for the cottage in the grounds of the Chapel, near its original site.

Marylou pedaled along on the lake trail, past some of the finest houses on the island, all with first class water views, past the delightful buildings and garden of the Society of the Four

Arts, past Palm Beach's oldest bridge, the Royal Park or Middle Bridge, where she crossed Royal Palm Way. After an admiring glance at the fine floating gin palaces along the docks, she turned left onto Peruvian Avenue to get to her gallery. There can be no better place on earth, Marylou mused almost every day when she parked her bike.

Seven years ago, on her father's death, Marylou had used her sizeable inheritance to fulfill a childhood dream. She managed to take over the lease of a lingerie shop that an old lady was ready to give up, and she opened an art gallery in one of the charming little shopping arcades built by Addison Mizner off Worth Avenue. At university she had run the gamut of constantly changing passions for a variety of periods, from medieval manuscript illuminations to Post Modernism, and from the earliest Italian masters to Pop Art. During her year in Florence, the Renaissance had completely captivated her. An apprenticeship at the Tate Gallery in London had awakened a deep appreciation for the great British painters, Constable, Gainsborough, Hogarth, and Turner.

To make her gallery a commercial success, she had to cater to the tastes and the demands of her customers, and in this she had succeeded. She still bought an occasional Old Master drawing or a contemporary work she fancied. However, for resale purposes she concentrated on minor painters from around the turn of the previous century, chose pleasant subjects and priced them sensibly. Her most ambitious purchases had been a couple of small oil paintings by William Glackens, the American impressionist, whom she much admired. They were so expensive that she had not found a buyer for them yet and, to tell the truth, she was happy to keep them as long as possible. As Marylou knew everybody, and was on excellent terms with the architects and designers of Palm Beach, they sent their own clients to her when their new houses were ready to be adorned with art work. It was not easy, but Marylou loved her job and made a reasonable living.

She had spent all her life in Palm Beach, but she was not a creature of South Florida. She was not a highlighted blond, pencil thin with a tanned body. Tall and strong-boned, she was athletic, and dressed plainly in dark trousers or longish skirts, simple tops, and comfortable flat shoes. Her greatest asset was her thick, long auburn hair, that she wore tied back or in a bun that tended to disintegrate before lunch time. She was not beautiful, but was extremely pleasant to look at, with her regular features, fine dark eyes and open expression.

Marylou was on her way to breakfast at Golfview Road to meet her old friend Sam Robertson. The two had grown up together, attended Palm Beach Day School, and had only parted when he went off to prep school in New England. Since going to Europe, she had not seen so much of Sam, but they had remained the best of friends, based on their shared upbringing, as well as their love for sports and art. They had never been lovers, rather, or so Marylou thought of them, "soul mates". Once Sam had wanted to be a painter and he would have been good at it, but then he had conformed (meekly, Marylou called it) to the family tradition and taken up law. Later they had dreamed of owning a gallery together. This also was not to be, but Sam had always shown the greatest interest in Marylou's business and every time he came back home, she was the first person he called to arrange a meeting. She loved her old friend deeply but sometimes she felt like shaking him to wake him up. "Stand up for yourself!" she wanted to say. "This is your life. Don't waste it!" In her eager anticipation to see Sam again, Marylou was much too early. It would take her just two minutes to bicycle to the Robertsons' house, breakfast was to be at nine o'clock and she had decided to wait here in this little garden for a while.

Marylou was often compared with her mother although—or because—the two could not be more different. Birdie, as Rosalind Baker was generally known, was in her fifties and still considered a beauty, with her wide blue eyes, almost unlined face and sun-streaked short hair. A size 4, she dressed in figure hugging cropped trousers and short, colorful shift dresses that set off her slim legs to perfection. ("For a woman, the last thing to go are the legs" was one of her mantras.) She gave such an impression of fragility that men instinctively jumped to her assistance. That she did not look a day older than forty was a compliment that she happily passed on to her cosmetic surgeon in Boca Raton and her dermatologist in the Poinciana Plaza.

Birdie often wondered how the dear God could have seen fit to give her a daughter who was so diametrically opposed to her in almost every way. Not that she did not love Marylou— she did, but she would have so adored having a little blond Shirley Temple for a daughter, whom she could have dressed up in cute little smocks and buckled shoes. Marylou took after her father, of course. Birdie conceded with a sigh that he had been a handsome man, but somehow his rugged masculinity had not mutated successfully, at least in Birdie's eyes, into a feminine version.

During the day Birdie wore tropical Lilly Pulitzer clothes, so beloved by Palm Beach ladies; Valentino or Chanel in the evening, teamed with her hallmark string of pearls. She could be rightly called a merry widow, because she looked with quiet satisfaction back to her married life and had settled equally contentedly into her new role as a single woman. Unlike some of her girlfriends, she was not looking for a new husband. Well, not anymore. There had once been a brief episode when romance raised its tempting head, when a meaningful relationship beckoned, when even another marriage seemed possible, but it had been the shortest of dreams, followed by a sobering, well, really quite painful awakening. Thankfully, utter discretion had prevailed, nobody knew—except Marylou, who may have guessed. Birdie had learned her lesson. Never, never again would she jeopardize her enjoyable, peaceful, uncomplicated life. Congenial, undemanding company, an attentive escort, when the occasion demanded a man at her side, was easily procured and that was all she asked for these days.

She was never bored ("Only boring people are bored" was another one of her mantras). The mornings were taken up with the usual maintenance jobs, hair, nails, massage, yoga etc. Then a light lunch, mostly with girlfriends, followed maybe by a rest, and then she did her rounds: checking out the merchandise along Worth Avenue and looking in on Marylou at her gallery. Mother and daughter shared a love of the arts, although in Birdie's case this was more or less exclusively reserved for an appreciation of the French impressionists. She approved of almost anything with a Gallic provenance... at least she used to. It was a source of some anxiety that Birdie felt, as a good American, she had to rein in her endorsement of all things French since the two countries' falling out over the Iraq war.

Occasionally Birdie visited the Norton Museum in West Palm Beach and, during the season, attended lectures at The Society of the Four Arts. They always covered interesting subjects, nothing too heavy, easily digested and forgotten. Other afternoons were spent playing bridge or canasta. Dinner often meant a party in one of her many friends' houses, or at one of the three clubs that circumscribed her social orbit: the Evergreen, the Bath and Tennis Club and Club Colette, a smart dining club on Peruvian Avenue that was particularly in demand among ladies who lunch, and some to whom membership in one of the former, more prestigious clubs was denied.

Today, at eight o'clock, Birdie sat at the breakfast table in her airy top floor apartment at the Brazilian, a smallish, popular, low key building in an enviable location: on Brazilian Avenue, just off South County Road and close to Town Hall. Breakfast could take up quite some time. Not that she ate much: Birdie had half a grapefruit, one slice of paper thin whole wheat toast with sugar-free orange marmalade and green tea. The Shiny Sheet kept her rooted to her place. Page one was of little interest ("Town Council discusses new zoning law"). Shannon Donnelly's society column, as always, held her undivided attention, describing in minutest detail parties that had been held weeks ago: who gave them, for what charity or occasion, who attended wearing what. On Wednesdays and Sundays the Social Calendar was an orgy of self-aggrandizement.

Of course there was no greater satisfaction than seeing oneself in the paper, confirming how popular and important one was. Some ladies, often with names flowery enough to come straight out of a Barbara Cartland novel, sat on every charity committee, attended bible classes and fashion parades, cocktail parties and trunk shows, parties to precede and conclude events, parties to thank, applaud and honor each other, and some ladies, as well as a few precious gentlemen, would happily attend the opening of an envelope as long as a photographer was present. Rumor had it that the repeated appearance of some ladies in print was not only due to their feverish social activities but to the employment of a public relations expert.

Charity had always been big in Palm Beach and enormous sums were given to many worthy causes. Genuine philanthropy blossomed thanks to a large number of clever and generous people who work tirelessly, but there was a side to this world that would not suit the fainthearted. Social climbing, disguised as altruism, seemed to bring out the devil in some. When an event was planned, or the postmortem was conducted, bickering, jealousy, even spite often ensued. What used to be a genteel hobby for "Lady Bountiful" had become a blood sport or, to paraphrase Oscar Wilde: "The pursuit of the unedifying by the unspeakable."

Every time Birdie spotted a familiar face on this roll call of maniacally smiling faces, she gave a little exclamation of delight or commiseration, depending on how flattering the photograph was. And there she was herself... in her pretty turquoise silk trousers from Trillion... at the cocktail party to launch next December's Bleeding Heart Ball for the Homeless... with her beau of the evening and the chairlady herself. Not bad, not bad at all. She must remember to get some copies of today's Shiny Sheet and cut out the article for her scrap book.

She was so excited, that she heard the door bell only when it rang for the second time. How interesting, she thought as she got up and quickly checked her appearance in a mirror. Visitors were rare at this hour.

* * *

At 8:45 Peggy and Martin Harris left their villa on Middle Road and got into the car to drive the short distance to Golfview Road for breakfast. Martin was a heavily built, tall man with a florid face and a shock of wiry grey hair.

He came from a family of early settlers in the Lake Worth area and had lived here all his life. He had a real estate license, but, as he never liked working for other people, he founded a construction company and now converted and built houses, sometimes for others, but mostly for himself, as a developer and speculator. His greatest coup had been the purchase of one of the huge late Mizner estates on South Ocean Boulevard. Nobody wanted this "white elephant" that needed an army of servants to keep going. But with skill, persuasion and infinite patience, Martin had succeeded in an adjustment of the town's zoning regulations that allowed him to divide the mansion into five apartments with shared gardens, beach access and pool. For once he had managed to keep his fiery temper in check, at least in all aspects concerning the project. He did a fine job, restoring the exterior to its former glory, while converting the interior into tasteful, luxurious spaces full of the latest technological sophistication. Despite their extravagant price tags the apartments sold well and made Martin a wealthy man. But this had happened more than ten years ago. Living the kind of carefree, easy life that he and Peggy enjoyed and had gotten used to, meant that the money was running out and the time had come to score again.

As Martin held the car door open for her, he looked fondly at Peggy. She was an unassuming woman, quite handsome in an understated way, reserved but intelligent company, and ran their home and social life with quiet efficiency. For a number of years she had worked as a realtor, as so many year-round Palm Beach residents did. In this small community, about a thousand people, more women than men, earned their money selling real estate. The competition was fierce, especially for "listings", but the rewards could be staggering. Properties changed hands continuously: houses were bought and enlarged or pulled down and replaced by bigger, more valuable buildings. The price of property, rising annually between 10 and 30%, was a topic of never-ending speculation and gloating. A fascination with the glorious and extravagant architecture of Palm Beach was a passion she shared with Martin.

Peggy had enjoyed working for Sotheby's and had only given it up a few years ago, reluctantly, when her ageing mother had moved in with them and needed her time and care. With her death, Peggy had lost the cutthroat edge that spelled success in real estate. Maybe one day she would go back to it, because she was certainly not without ambition. What mere acquaintances did not know was, that behind Peggy's gentle and genteel manner lay a steely determination. Husband and wife aimed for the same target, but where Martin bustled noisily forward, Peggy treaded softly and advanced all the faster.

They had only just emerged from their separate bed rooms. Martin was a notoriously early riser who usually started the day well before his wife, who was a bad sleeper and liked to be left undisturbed in the morning.

It took them just a few minutes to drive down South County Road. At the Colony Hotel they turned left onto Worth Avenue and left again at the Evergreen Club, toward the parking lot and the golf pavilion, and left again onto Golfview Road. Deep in thought, Martin parked his car outside the Robertson mansion. (Private Road! Parking only for Residents!) What an exquisite building it is, and so enormous, he mused. When would Frank decide that it was too big for him? Sheila and Bill would never live there. Sam showed no sign of wanting to get married and anyway, who could afford the expensive upkeep in the long run, and pay huge property taxes, both rising steadily every year?

The main house, built in a U-shape, could easily be divided into three units and then there were the garage block and the servants' quarters. Peggy looked pensively at her husband as he slowly parked the car. She knew what was going through his head. She smiled and briefly put her hand on his that still rested on the steering wheel. It was time to go in.

CHAPTER 4

At 8:30 a.m. sharp, Molly Miller left her condominium at 325 South Ocean Boulevard to keep her appointment at the Evergreen Club. She strode out with short, determined steps in her disproportionately large white sneakers. They looked incongruous with the elegant clothes she always wore: today it was a little pale blue suit with a matching bow-tie silk blouse. The sneakers were Mrs. Miller's concession to exercise, deemed so indispensable in Palm Beach. Instead of driving her car, she walked eagerly in the vicinity of the town, but in order to abide by her self-set rules of acceptable attire, she carried her little high-heel pumps around with her in a carrier bag and as soon as the place or occasion demanded it, she changed from sneakers into pumps and vice versa.

The Evergreen Club, in particular the golf pavilion—recently renamed the Palm Terrace—was home away from home for Molly Miller. At age seventy-two, she was a sprightly woman of pleasing proportions. Well under medium height, she had curves where they were supposed to be—this is how her much missed late husband, Jim Miller, used to describe her. She still had the brown curly hair of her youth (with the help of Jean-Christophe, the best "hair artist" in town) and merry hazel eyes. Her taste in clothes had hardly changed over the last thirty years. She favored neatly tailored two-piece suits in pastel colors, her comfortable bosom ensconced in charmingly feminine blouses.

After an unhappy first marriage, entered into when she was "a mere child", she was left a desolate divorcée… for a few months. She met Jim on the golf course in Cleveland and that was it. They had both felicitously run into their ideal partner. She personified his idea of perfect womanhood, beautiful to his eye, soft to his hands, and endlessly willing to listen to the stories of his hunting, shooting, fishing and golfing prowess. In return he idolized, pampered and spoiled her furiously, "Molly-coddling" he had called it. She was indulged and petted, and they reveled in each other's company. When in Palm Beach, Jim Miller's daily occupation had been a round of golf at the Evergreen Club. In their first years together, Molly had joined him. After she had given up playing, due to a shoulder injury, she still made the clubhouse her daytime residence. From there, Molly had waved her husband off to the course and three hours later was there to welcome him back.

With his passing away, Molly saw no reason to change her routine. Very sadly, there was no Jim to kiss good bye and hello, but there were still many dear friends to see, to join for meals, or for a hand of bridge. In clement weather she sat on the patio, shaded by umbrellas or a tree; when it turned too hot or cold, Molly moved inside to the ladies' locker room or the library, with its charming palm tree murals. Soft armchairs beckoned her to sit and read a book, and there were plenty of desks and tables on which to write letters or play patience.

More formal events took place in the main building of the club, which was a picture of medieval Spanish elegance—tastefully updated for modern comfort. Antique tiles, elaborate wooden doors and ceilings and huge potted trees created an atmosphere of romantic grandeur. In the vast dining room, the roof slid back over the dance floor. Molly remembered dreamily the parties when Jim, who was at least a keen, if not great dancer, whirled her around under a starry sky.

When the occasion demanded, she darted across the road, to see the new summer dresses at Isabel's, to order embroidered linen napkins from Mary Mahoney or buy some shoes from Stubbs & Wootton. Her furthest ports of call were the Society of the Four Arts on Royal Palm Avenue and her hairdresser in the Royal Poinciana Plaza. These were occasions for Molly Miller to don her walking shoes and stride out gamely. When kind friends took her to the Norton Museum or the Kravis Center, Molly felt excited. Crossing the bridge to go to West Palm was like an expedition into a foreign country. But like a boomerang she was always pulled back into the comforting cocoon of the Evergreen Club, until it was time to go home, often just to change clothes and return for an evening engagement.

Today there was a special, eager spring in Molly's step. She was looking forward to having breakfast with her old friend Lucy de Silva, who had arrived in Palm Beach four days earlier. She had appeared out of the blue to present herself to Molly and they had been inseparable ever since.

The two ladies were childhood friends but had lost touch after Lucy and her family had moved away from Cleveland, when they were in their twenties. Although they had been separated for so long, their recent reunion had been a huge success. They had taken up, it seems, just where they had left off almost fifty years earlier.

"Good morning, Mrs. Miller." The receptionist opened the heavy glass door and led their early guest into the golf pavilion. "Inside or out?" she wanted to know.

"I think outside, Edna, dear," murmured Molly. "Such a beautiful morning!" She chose one of the white armchairs at a table well shaded by the magnificent ficus tree that dominated the patio of the Evergreen Club golf pavilion. From where she sat, Molly had a clear view towards the glass doors through which she expected to see her guest arrive, as well as over the driving range, the putting green and the pro shop. Even before the waiter brought her the menu and ice water, she had already surreptitiously changed her shoes under the table. Shod in her white pumps, sneakers stowed away, Molly Miller was ready for her friend.

Within minutes the doors swung open and with the audible click-clack that the heavy metal feet of her crutches made on the stone floor, Lucy de Silva advanced. Lucy had the same pretty brown eyes as Molly. Although taller and more youthful looking, she suffered from the afflictions brought on by a childhood bout of polio. Her legs had been so weakened that she could only walk with the help of crutches. This, however, she managed so skillfully and with such little fuss that people in her company quickly forgot that she was less than mobile. Molly remembered that even as a young woman she had never displayed a hint of bitterness or self pity and had always remained active and independent.

Molly jumped up with a little cry of delight to embrace her. "Lucy, my dearest! I am so happy to see you. It is just wonderful that you can make your own way over here from the hotel. You must be exhausted." With the help of the headwaiter she settled her friend comfortably in one of the chairs, resting the crutches between another chair and the table. "Let me spoil you," Molly carried on. "Shall we start with some fresh orange juice or half a grapefruit? I hope you're hungry."

Lucy did indeed look rather flushed and hot despite the early hour. She had strong, well-chiseled features and sported a short, sensible haircut that suited her. To hide her withered legs she usually wore slacks, thin khaki trousers in this tropical climate, and a colorfully embroidered white cotton shirt, tucked into her waistband.

She smiled at her friend. "You mustn't worry about me, you know. I think I can say in all honesty that I have come to terms with my two "irons" long ago, emotionally as well as physically. I am in great shape apart from these boring old legs and you see, I even outlived Lily, who was, after all five years younger, fit and healthy, and should by rights have survived me."

The ladies had already swapped family news on the first day of their reunion. Both sets of parents were dead of course, but Molly had been saddened and surprised to learn that Lucy's younger sister, Lily, had been killed in a car crash five years earlier. As if this were not upsetting enough, Lucy had to confess that her niece Gail, Lily's only child, had also died, quite recently. Although no details were divulged, Molly had somehow formed the impression that drugs, possibly in combination with drink, had been the cause. Nobody knew the whereabouts of Gail's father, Lily's husband. After a short-lived marriage he had moved to Europe and in due course was never heard of again.

"We must be so grateful to be alive, to be together and in such a gorgeous place as Palm Beach," sighed Mrs. Miller. "I hope you can stay a long time. There is so much I want to show you. The island is very small, but utterly delightful and there is a lot to do, especially if you play bridge or at least backgammon."

She hesitated. "You do play? Maybe a little Canasta or Rummy?" She was almost pleading.

Lucy smiled. "Yes I do, don't worry. And for the next three or four days I am totally at your disposal, with or without cards, but next week I will have to leave you. There is some business I have to take care of."

"Oh Lucy, dearest, you are so clever." Molly's face was wreathed in genuine admiration. "I am afraid I am absolutely useless for any sort of business, especially when long rows of numbers are involved. Thank God, Jim left all his affairs in good order and I have an accountant who takes care of everything. It still puzzles me that we both studied physics and chemistry in 6th grade rather than art and French like your sister. Nowadays anything financial or scientific is quite beyond me."

"Maybe the reason was the handsome science teacher, Mr. Murdoch. Wasn't that his name?" suggested Lucy. They both laughed.

For some time, their waitress, Rose, had been hovering patiently at a discreet distance, ready to take their orders.

Molly remembered her duties as a hostess and quickly made some suggestions. "The omelettes here are very good, but so is the French toast. I can also recommend the croissants and when I am very naughty I order the sticky pecan buns. Utterly delicious and wicked! Each one has about 2,000 calories but they are worth it. And anyway, you are so slim. I am the one who should be careful." She giggled. "But not always. After all, there are not many sins left for us to commit."

Rose had barely taken their order when all three became aware of some commotion outside the pro shop. Then they heard the police siren and an ambulance driving up to the club.

Molly looked around in surprise. "Heavens to Betsy! Whatever happened? Do you think one of the old boys overdid it on the golf course? That might explain an ambulance, but what are the police doing here?"

She turned to the head waiter. He shook his head and offered to go off to make inquiries. Mrs. Miller took stock of the situation. "Well, I think we'll carry on with breakfast. Police and ambulances can only mean bad things, and we'll hear about them soon enough."

By 9:15 the Robertson household was on full alert. The impossible had happened: Frank had not returned from his round of golf on time. Breakfast had to be delayed. Family and guests were waiting in the garden room.

Marjorie had taken up a vantage position at a window on the second floor overlooking the short drive that led from Golfview Road to the house. The butler could barely maintain his usual cool demeanor. He had given orders to the kitchen to hold all further preparations. He offered juice and coffee to everybody in the room. As soon as they were all served, he started walking nervously between hall and garden room, listening for advancing steps. The police siren could only be heard as a distant sound because cars reached the Evergreen Club from Worth Avenue. Marylou, Sam and Gil stood together at the open terrace door, talking animatedly. Morreen nursed a cup of ginger and celery tea. As even decaf coffee was rejected by her group of health fanatic friends, she traveled with her own supply of life-preserving herbs, grains and powders from Planet Organic.

Maurice had not blinked an eyelid the night before, when Morreen pressed the paper bag full of strong-smelling leaves into his hand and informed him of her dietary requirements: herbal tea for breakfast, after lunch and dinner, otherwise Badoit or another table water with very small bubbles.

Sheila sat silently on a sofa, hands demurely folded in her lap. She watched her husband exchange pleasantries with Peggy and Martin Harris. She suppressed a sigh but could not prevent tears rising to her eyes. Half an hour earlier, she and Bill had had a nasty scene.

When he finally came home—from wherever he had been—she was so upset and tense that all caution flew out of the window. In a shrill voice she had demanded to know why he had left so early and where he had been. In response, Bill had just stared at her and then replied icily that he was hardly obliged to give her an account of his movements. Hurt by his tone as much as his words, she had burst into tears. Instead of taking her into his arms, as he would have done some years ago, he had asked her harshly to stop crying.

"Dammit woman, you wanted to come here—what's the matter now? I thought you enjoyed being with your family. As for me—I hope you don't expect me to spend all my time inside these four walls. You know I don't like your father. I could well have done without this visit, and if you go on like this, we might as well pack up and leave." Never before had they spoken to each other like that, and Sheila wondered what in the world was going to happen to them.

It was young Willie, the last one to emerge from his room, bleary-eyed and still adjusting his clothes, who suggested action.

"Dad, shall I go over to the club and look for Grandpa?"

Bill looked up and over to his wife. "What? Oh yes, good idea. See, what's going on."

* * *

When Willie arrived at the club house, the golf manager recognized him and called him over to the policemen. They

58

talked to him briefly and then the officer walked him back to No. 7 Golfview Road.

Ten minutes later a pale-looking Willie came back to the house, accompanied by a tall policeman in uniform who introduced himself as Officer Fleming.

After a second's stunned silence, everybody started talking together, asking questions, all at once. The officer lifted both hands to ask for silence. "Just a moment, please. I understand this is Mr. Francis Robertson's house…"

Sam interrupted him. "Yes, and I am his son. My name is Sam Robertson. This is my sister Sheila, her husband Bill, and their son, Willie you know.

"Over there is my late mother's brother, Gillian Fellows, with his girlfriend, Morreen." Sam continued around the room, pointing out and introducing everybody in the assembled group.

"These are three friends of the family: Marylou Baker and Martin and Peggy Harris." He glanced briefly over to Marcel Dutroix, who kept discreetly in the background, and then decided to omit further introductions. "Please tell us what happened! Where is my father? Did he have an accident?"

The officer cleared his throat nervously. "I am afraid so. Someone found him lying on the ground. The ambulance has taken him to the hospital in West Palm Beach."

"Is he alright?" Sheila asked in a shrill voice. "I mean, he is not… dead, is he?"

"I am so sorry," answered the policeman gravely. "There was nothing the paramedics could do for him. When we got to him, he was already dead."

"Oh my God," exclaimed Peggy Harris and her hands flew to her mouth.

Sam moved to his sister, who had jumped up from the sofa, and put a comforting arm around her shoulder. "Was it a heart attack?" he wanted to know.

"No," said the officer. He hesitated for a moment and then carried on. "I am sorry to bring you further bad news, but it looks as if Mr. Robertson may have met with foul play. It is too early in our investigation to say for sure, but it looks as if he may have been the victim of a blunt force injury. I shouldn't tell you this, but he may have been bludgeoned with a golf club."

The women in the room shrieked as if with one voice. "Oh my God," repeated Mrs. Harris and sank onto an armchair.

"But that's just not possible," whispered Sheila. "Who would do such a horrible thing?"

"We don't know yet," answered the policeman. "But the Chief has the area secured, and has road blocks set up on the bridges."

Marylou, although badly shaken, had managed to pull herself together. She turned to Sheila. "Would you like to lie down? Shall I go upstairs with you?"

Sheila, whose eyes had filled with tears, nodded silently. The two women left the room, Marylou leading the way.

Officer Fleming turned to the remaining group. "Obviously we have no idea at present who might have committed this crime, but I assure you, we, the Palm Beach police force, will do our very best to find the murderer. I am afraid we will have to ask you all some questions. None of you will be leaving Palm Beach in the next few days, I trust?" Everybody shook his head.

"I have to go now. The sergeant will come by shortly to take down your details so we'll know how we can get in touch with you. It is likely that a higher-ranking officer from the crime squad in West Palm Beach or Fort Lauderdale will handle the case." He looked around and his eyes rested on Sam.

"I am sorry. This is a terrible thing to have happened. Our pathologist is examining your father as we speak, to find out when exactly, and how, he was killed. Later today you can see your father at the morgue and make further arrangements." With these words he nodded and turned around to leave.

* * *

Molly and Lucy had not quite managed to forget that something was happening outside the pro shop, but they were busy filling in the gaps that their fifty-odd year separation had left.

"Jim was the perfect husband," Molly remembered dreamily. "My first husband had left me quite disillusioned with men... and frankly, my dear, if you look around, nowadays there is very little marriage material—in quality and quantity. Men have it made for themselves, especially here. No matter how poor and unattractive they may be—as long as they can still walk unaided, they are a hit. In my experience, if they're not gay, they are only interested in 'nurse or purse'. I was very lucky with my Jim. He was the perfect gentleman..."

Molly was drifting off into her blissful memories, as the headwaiter advanced with a tall policeman in tow, clearly aiming for their table.

"Mrs. Miller, this is Detective Fleming who would like a word with you." With this introduction he withdrew discreetly.

"Good morning, Mrs. Miller," the officer began. "I am sorry to disturb you and your friend..." As expected, Molly introduced her friend and invited Fleming to sit down with them.

"Officer, can you tell us what happened? We saw the ambulance and the police car and naturally, we are worried. Was there an accident?"

"I am afraid so, Mrs. Miller," answered Fleming. "The news will get around quickly enough, so I might as well tell you. Mr. Francis Robertson, I believe you know him, has been murdered and poor Mr. Harvey found him on the golf course, which was quite a shock for him, as you can imagine. I understand you ladies have been sitting here for a while. From this table you have a fairly good view over to the pro shop, the putting green, even the driving range and the caddy house. Can you tell me what or whom you saw this morning?"

"Oh my God, Detective, what a ghastly thing to have happened... here of all places! I'm in shock. Of course I know Frank Robertson... I mean, I knew him. I have been acquainted with him and his family for many years. You see, this place is like my second home and I know all the regular golfers and most of the people who live on Golfview Road. I don't think my friend can help you. She only arrived in Palm Beach a few days ago. She is a complete stranger here and doesn't know a soul apart from me. Isn't that right, Lucy, dear?" Mrs. de Silva nodded her assent.

Molly Miller was now in full flow and carried on: "Now, let me think. I didn't see Frank at all this morning. He always starts his round of golf around eight, well before I arrived, which was about a quarter of nine. I would have expected to see him return around this time, but Lucy arrived shortly after I did and obviously I wasn't paying much attention to what was happening in the golf cart and pro shop area... until the commotion started, that is. I seem to remember that I noticed Osbert setting off around the same time that our scrambled eggs arrived. Some other people returned... nobody I recognized or remember though."

"Thank you, Mrs. Miller, that is all I need to know at the moment. If you remember anything else that could be important, please call me. Here is my card—or drop in at the police station. I have to go back now. I know where you live, just in case we want to get in touch with you. And you, Mrs. de Silva, where are you staying? You won't be leaving Palm Beach today or tomorrow, I hope?"

"I have a room at the Colony Hotel," answered Lucy, "and I will be here until Wednesday at least."

"Thank you, ladies. I wish you, despite everything, a pleasant day." With these words Officer Fleming took his leave.

"And you described Palm Beach as an oasis of peace and quiet to me," protested Lucy in mock horror as the officer departed. "Who is, or rather who was, this Frank Robinson?"

"Robertson, Frank Robertson," corrected Molly. "I promise you, for forty odd years this place has seen no crime worse than a stolen bicycle. And now a murder at the Evergreen Golf Club! Heavens to Betsy! Well, Frank is not really a friend of mine, rather an acquaintance. I liked his wife very much, but she died a few years ago. He has two rather nice children, a boy, he must be about thirty now, who lives in New York, I believe, and a daughter, slightly older, who is married and lives in Ohio or Pennsylvania, I don't remember. His house is just over there on Golfview Road. It's a beautiful property, original Wyeth, on a big double lot, fabulous gardens... a real gem."

"Do you think he was robbed?" asked Lucy de Silva. "I mean, would someone have murdered him for... I don't know... his watch, or the money he carried with him or whatever?"

"Unlikely," mused Molly. "He might have possessed a valuable wrist watch but he probably would not have carried a lot of cash with him around on the golf course... No, no, there must be a different motive. Of course, I imagine he will be leaving quite a bit of money behind. So the reason could be greed or hate or revenge for something. One sometimes hears about what the French call a "crime passionel" —but somehow I guess this is not the case here. An irate husband taking revenge for the seduction of his wife? No, no. Maybe money was behind it, but he would not have been killed for it by a stranger. Whoever did this must have known him... and his habits... and must somehow have gained entry to the golf course. I daresay this is not an ordinary hit, grab and run case. The killer prepared his assault and he must have had a powerful motive. Lucy, dear, I just hope you are not too shocked or frightened."

Lucy de Silva shook her head. "Certainly not. It is dreadfully sad, but these things happen occasionally and I don't expect there will be a mass outbreak of killings in Palm Beach. I am quite sure your police department is very efficient and the whole thing is going to be solved in no time at all."

Molly sighed and signaled to the waitress to sign the chit. "I'll tell you what, Lucy. Let's sit here for a little longer and then go to the Mouse which will open at ten. That will distract us and take our mind off the murder."

Lucy looked up in surprise. "The 'Mouse'? Do explain!"

Molly laughed "Sorry, dear. I neglected so far to introduce you to one of the island's greatest institutions. The Church Mouse, to give it its proper name, is a very superior second hand shop for clothes, household articles, books etc. It is run as a charity by volunteers in aid of the local church, Bethesda-by-the-Sea. And if you think, second hand clothes sound horrid, think again. This is the place where everybody goes to find a bargain. Many people in Palm Beach don't like to be seen wearing some of their clothes, especially evening attire, more than once or maybe twice, and so the most glorious designer gowns can be picked up 'for a song', as well as tailored suits, bags, shoes, scarves, fashion jewelry, anything you can think of.

"Everything is, of course, perfectly clean. The other day I found the most adorable peach-colored ensemble. Unfortunately I have no top to go with this and I would love to go back and see what they have in today. The shop is nearby, on the corner of County Road and Chilean Avenue, a pretty pink building. Maybe you have seen it?" Lucy shook her head.

"Do you think you can walk that far?" Molly wanted to know.

"Absolutely no problem, Molly. You must get used to the idea that I am almost perfectly mobile. Let's go. This sounds like a great idea! I don't think I will look for a ball gown but maybe some cotton shirts or light weight trousers would be useful."

At this moment a middle-aged, attractive looking couple passed their table and gave Molly a friendly nod, a greeting that was returned by her with a cheerful wave.

Molly leaned forward and whispered confidentially: "The lady, who just walked by, is quite a celebrity with us. She is our former mayor, Lyndsy Jones, and jolly good she was too: well-informed, decisive, independent and not afraid to speak her mind. Such a pity, she would not run for office again, although the new man, her successor, is highly regarded too.

"The gentleman with her is the Honorable Charles Benton, a member of the British aristocracy. I understand he is something like a distant cousin or uncle to poor dear Diana, the Princess of Wales. But Charles has been living here in Florida with us for a very long time. Being single and a good bridge player, he is extremely popular. He has started organizing Scottish dancing lessons and I have been to some of them. I tell you, these reels, that's what they call the dances, are not easy to learn. You have to concentrate frightfully or you end up in a dreadful muddle, grabbing the wrong partner, going off in the wrong direction. Dear me...!" She shook her head with a little laugh. "I even managed to talk my friend Henry Standing into joining. We had so much fun.

"After Henry I think Charlie is the most popular single man in Palm Beach, so much in demand. You see, there are just too many women on their own," she added wistfully. "We need presentable walkers, as we call them, respectable gentlemen to accompany us to social events. Without them, a lot of women would not be going anywhere. Usually they are very charming. They appreciate a new hair style or dress and are often far better company than some boorish husband."

Lucy smiled at her friend's animation. "For such a small place, Palm Beach really has a lot to offer, charming walkers and even Scottish square dancing."

"Ha," interjected Molly triumphantly, "and I have not even launched properly into island politics. The hottest iron is probably the rescue of landmarks or historically important houses. The preservation of buildings that their owners want to pull down or divide and sell piecemeal, is a subject that makes people really hot under the collar.

"A lovely mansion built by the famous Maurice Fatio was recently demolished, although it was clearly a landmark. The new owner wanted to add another story and asked for permission which was, surprisingly, granted. However, this resulted in the whole building being pulled down, apparently due to a misunderstanding or lack of communication between him, his architect and the town planning department. Suddenly there was this huge outcry, but the dastardly deed was done. And as usual, nobody took the blame. I tell you, the things that go on

66

here…" Her voice trailed off. Molly was clearly in her element. Gossip, local events, preferably tinged with a whiff of scandal, were her life.

CHAPTER 5

SATURDAY

"Mr. Harvey's Residence," announced a smooth male voice over the intercom.

"My name is Gonzalez, Special Agent in Charge Gonzalez, from the West Palm Beach office of the FBI. I'm here to speak to Mr. Harvey."

"One moment, please, Sir."

The heavy glass door at No. 9 Golfview Road swung silently open. 'The Towers', built in 1927 by Maurice Fatio, was a solid-looking two-story house with a massive tower and numerous quasi-Spanish stylistic elements: heavy stone lintels, rustic wooden shutters and wrought-iron lamps and grilles.

The butler, dressed in an immaculate dark suit with silver tie, examined the agent's credentials, and ushered the visitor into the house.

Agent Gonzalez was a big man, somewhere in his forties, with a droopy moustache and sorrowful eyes. His solemn expression was so much in demand during his working life that it had become permanently fixed. He wore a dark linen suit, a little crumpled, with a rather surprising pink tie. If the truth were to be told, Emilio Gonzalez was more than a little self-conscious about this colorful addition to his otherwise conventional outfit. His wife, Teresa, who had bought him the tie, had insisted that he wear it today. And Teresa was not a woman to be trifled with.

Gonzalez had always cultivated a nonthreatening air of physical and mental slowness, which was quite misleading. His Latin origins—he was second generation Columbian—were less of a handicap working for a Federal agency than they would have been within a local police department dominated by "Anglo" personnel. He was well aware that his precipitous assignment to this case was bound to raise eyebrows and cause friction with the local authority figures, but he was a diligent, competent, methodical agent who had learned long ago that it paid to keep an open mind, to listen patiently, and not to jump to conclusions.

He followed the butler into a first, smallish reception room, overlooking the courtyard. There was a stone staircase on one side, leading upstairs and downstairs. Straight ahead loomed another, larger sitting room and to the right what appeared to be a formal dining room. The rooms were white-washed, with high wooden ceilings and ornate furniture of vaguely European provenance. The agent noted large family portraits in heavy gilt frames and thick oriental carpets.

Before he had time to look around further, an elderly man came down the stairs to greet him. Although likely to be over seventy, he was youthful looking, whippet-thin and of military bearing. His thinning hair was tightly brushed over his head, his well-chiseled face smooth and tanned. He was dressed in sharply pressed grey trousers and a vivid turquoise-colored silk shirt which even to the agent's fashion-blind eyes looked tailor made and expensive.

Gonzalez remembered what his sources had told him about Osbert Harvey: He was the scion of a wealthy Virginian family and enjoyed the luxury of devoting himself to the pursuit of a sophisticated social life. In this he had accomplished much. Nobody organized tennis and golf games, luncheons, dinner and dances like Osbert Harvey. His speciality was his chocolate and champagne parties, which nobody declined. They were, like all his gatherings, hugely successful because Osbert cared about his friends and took enormous trouble to make them feel welcome. With his impeccable social graces and infectious joie de vivre, he well deserved his nickname: 'Mr. Palm Beach'.

He shook the agent's hand and introduced himself. "I am Osbert Harvey and I imagine you want to talk to me about poor old Francis. I already gave a statement to the local police yesterday, but I am perfectly willing to tell you everything again.

"Please, do sit down!" He pointed to a sofa. With the refined manners of a bygone age, he made sure that his visitor was comfortably seated and offered him a cold drink.

"I am sure, you are highly qualified and the best person to deal with this case, but would you mind telling me why our Palm Beach police force has not been entrusted with this murder?"

Gonzalez took up the glass the butler had handed him. "Thank you. Well, I am attached to the West Palm Beach satellite office of the FBI's Miami Field Office, and under certain special circumstances, a homicide in Florida is sometimes assigned to us. This is no reflection at all on your capable officers here in Palm Beach."

He took a sip and carried on. "Mr. Harvey, I read your statement and would like to know whether there is anything you can add to this. Have you remembered any other details?"

"I am afraid not. But let's go over it again. Where was I? Well, I got up quite early, I am a bad sleeper these days, you know. I took a long shower, shaved, did my exercises… do you exercise, Agent Gonzalez?" Emilio shook his head regretfully.

"Frightfully important as you get older. Of course, you are still a young man, compared to me." Osbert Harvey sighed deeply.

"So, I had a demi-cup of very strong coffee, Kenyan. I have my own blend, made exclusively from coffee plants grown on the upper slopes of the Aberdare Hills. You must try my coffee one day. The flavor is incomparable. But I transgress... or is that digress?... Where were we?"

"You had your coffee," the agent interjected. "And then you went to the golf course?"

"No, no, first I visited Mother to wish her a good morning. She is a teensy weensy bit grumpy first thing, I must confess, but I always try my best to jolly her up." Mr. Harvey looked so glum that Gonzalez had the impression that these morning visits might conceivably be quite a test even for Osbert Harvey's filial devotion. He pulled himself visibly together.

"Yes, then I crossed the road, took a cart and started playing—the back nine holes that is—at about nine o'clock. I had barely gotten into my swing, near the 10th hole, when I found the golf bag and then the body." He shuddered at the memory. "Dear, oh dear, it was gruesome.

"If my ball had not landed in that area, nobody would have found him for a while. He was sort of hidden by some shrubs. As you know he was lying face down, the back of his head was all bloody. One iron club, I think it was his sand wedge, was right next to the body, covered in blood. A terrible sight! The poor man! At the time I didn't know, of course, it was Francis. I just jumped into my cart and drove back like the devil to get help. Not that I thought he might still be alive. You wouldn't have a chance to survive with your head bashed in like that.

"Tell me, Agent Gonzalez, do you think we have a psychopath here in Palm Beach or a sociopath, if that's the word?

Now that the FBI is involved... I'm pondering the political implications. Maybe there was a conspiracy of foreign powers? The Russians? Or the Koreans? A white collar crime connection? Is that it? I'd better not tell Mother about it. Should we take special precautions to protect ourselves, particularly at night? I once read an article on copycat murders." He seemed genuinely worried.

Once again Agent Gonzalez' habitually doleful expression matched the severity of the situation. "Frankly, I don't expect another murder, but of course precautions are always good. Just carry on as before and use your common sense."

He paused for a moment, expecting another anxiety attack from his host, but when none came he continued: "Tell me, how well did you know the deceased? Did he have enemies? I understand you have lived here a long time. Can you think of anyone who would want him dead?"

"Goodness gracious, no! Enemies? Well now, that's a strong word. Let's just say that Francis had a strong personality and was not a very popular man. There is no point in beating about the bush. For instance, there was no love lost between him and Frederick Brownlow, the president of the Evergreen Club. If I recall correctly, there were tensions between the two men right from the time the Robertsons moved here, almost thirty years ago. I don't remember whether they had known each other previously. But it was an open secret that they did not get on and sort of avoided each other. Why? I have no idea.

"I doubt that you will get anything out of Frederick. He is a cold fish. Sorry, I shouldn't say that. Let me rephrase that: he is a perfect gentleman, but he just has no interest in anything apart from golf. The Evergreen Club is his life. He used to be a member of The Old Guard golf and bridge club, but he found it too time-consuming and resigned, in order to devote himself totally to the Evergreen. Can't imagine what he did with himself before they made him president. Mind you, he is bloody good at it, revels in the attention and the power. And I must admit he is very generous, pays for a lot of things that other presidents would charge to the club. He is not married, never has been, as far as I know. He lives in this grand house of his, alone with a string of staff. Obviously there are no money worries. Lucky man! It's shockingly expensive to keep these monstrous houses from crumbling."

He sighed wistfully, thereby indicating that he himself was not in such a lucky position. Compared to his wealthy neighbors, Osbert Harvey considered himself a pauper. But then, money was such a relative thing: someone regarded as poor in Palm Beach would be called rich anywhere else in the world.

Special Agent in Charge Gonzalez, his face wreathed in commiseration, waited patiently while his host rambled on about his unreasonable financial restrictions. Gonzalez knew that a lot of seemingly irrelevant talk often contains some information that might prove to be important. He used the time to look around him, at the sizeable rooms, so comfortably appointed. Mr. Harvey might feel hard up, but to a man with a fixed salary, like Gonzalez, his life style seemed enviable.

"And now, since the hurricane, things are worse than ever. You have no idea, how badly this house was damaged. We had water everywhere, and would you believe it, the tower room is still m-o-i-s-t." The last word was spelt letter by letter which caused Gonzalez to look up with an expression of baffled disbelief.

His host noticed and smiled. "You are too young, Agent Gonzalez, but I was brought up with the notion that certain words are not to be used in polite society. Never mind, I guess I am one of a dying breed."

Gonzalez made a mental note to bring this interesting subject to Teresa's attention later that night and forced himself to carry on with his interrogation.

"May I ask who lives here? Whoever committed this crime must know this neighborhood and Mr. Robertson's daily routine. That's why we hope you and all the other residents will help us with our investigation."

"Why, certainly! Apart from myself, there is only Vincent, who is our butler, cook, bottle washer, handyman… name it, he does it. We are very lucky to have him. And then there is a nurse looking after Mother, but they are constantly changing and this is organized by an agency in West Palm."

Osbert Harvey looked up, suddenly animated. "But you haven't met Mother! Do come and say hello! She so loves receiving callers, especially gentlemen. She will be very pleased to see you."

Before Gonzalez had time to answer, his host had jumped up and led him up the stairs and along a corridor. He knocked briefly on a door, and beckoning the special agent to follow him, entered the room. There, in an armchair, sat Mrs. Aline Settrup, once the reigning social queen of Palm Beach. Now, aged ninety-three, she was still a handsome woman. Her nurse had dressed her in crème-colored silk trousers and a pink top, giving proper attention to matching jewelry and shoes. Her white hair was still full and was neatly arranged, her face carefully made up, with plenty of powder and just a touch too much rouge. Mrs. Settrup was clearly ready to receive.

Before coming to the Harvey residence, the agent had made some enquiries about the murdered man's immediate neighbors. Mrs. Settrup appeared to be known to everybody, but more by rumor and reputation than actual acquaintance. Her most striking accomplishment seemed to be the fact that she was a much married lady. She had started early, running away with one of her father's friends when she was just eighteen. Even her son Osbert was uncertain whether he, the first born, had had five or six stepfathers over the years. What everybody agreed upon, however, was that she was blessed with great beauty, some of which she may have lost, and a considerable fortune, which she still controlled. Osbert, who had never married, doted on his mother and was the most considerate, helpful, loving son imaginable. He had adapted their house with chair lifts, ramps and a wheelchair-friendly bathroom to make life as pleasant as possible for his mother. No husband could have been more considerate (and none had been) than Osbert, who chose her clothes, took her to the hairdresser and organized her little ladies' luncheons.

There were younger siblings from different fathers, but relations between them all had not always been easy. Mrs. Settrup, despite her failing health, was still a force to be reckoned with. At ninety-three she presided in frail but unquestionable majesty over her household. She got irritable at the slightest provocation and often threatened to change her will when her whims were not indulged. Among other considerations there was an enormous amount of jewelry which she could leave to anyone she chose. She was well aware of the power she wielded, which did nothing to soften her demanding nature. She was imperious in her manner, dictatorial despite her fragility, and not overburdened with delicacy of feelings and language towards anyone, least of all her son Osbert.

On seeing Special Agent in Charge Gonzalez, she gave him a dazzling, coquettish smile. Her son made the introduction and she stretched out a papery hand with brightly painted nails to greet her visitor. Without hesitation, and to his own surprise, Gonzalez found himself bowing over the frail hand and feigning a chivalrous kiss. Gonzalez realized that there was no point in continuing his interrogation here and decided to get this unexpected social encounter over with as quickly as possible.

"I am always so thrilled when Osbert brings his friends to see me," she murmured. "And how is your dear mother?"

Gonzalez, clearly taken back, answered truthfully that she was very well indeed and in return enquired after Mrs. Settrup's health. She complained about numbness in her legs, occasional dizzy spells and went into a detailed description of a stabbing pain in her chest. Having listened patiently for a few minutes, Gonzalez, aware of the time, finally got up and prepared to take his leave. Mrs. Settrup, tired by such an unexpectedly eventful morning, waved a gracious goodbye and begged him to remember her to his dear mother.

Downstairs, Gonzalez turned to Harvey. "You have been most kind, Mr. Harvey, thank you very much for sparing me your time. It was a pleasure to meet Mrs. Settrup. I am afraid I have to carry on with further interviews." With these words he took his leave.

* * *

Peggy Harris mixed the salad dressing just the way Martin liked it: two-thirds olive oil, one-third balsamic vinegar, some Dijon mustard, a pinch of sugar and plenty of basil. She shook the jar and poured its content over the salad she had prepared. After thirty-six years of marriage Martin still chose to come home for lunch whenever possible. She took the bread rolls from the oven. Should she mention what kept going through her mind? They did not really have secrets from each other, but something made her hesitate to bring up what had been bothering and preoccupying her all day. Where had Martin been yesterday morning? She was such a light sleeper that even his careful steps on the gravel had woken her up. He had not mentioned to her any early morning engagement, yet there he was, before eight o'clock, fully dressed, not in exercise clothes, sneaking out of the house. That was the only way to describe it. He had come back less than thirty minutes later, but neglected to mention that he had already been out when he and Peggy set off together to see Frank. Very odd... very odd indeed.

* * *

It was three o'clock in the afternoon when Molly Miller returned home to 325 South Ocean Boulevard. It was not an architecturally remarkable building, virtually none of the apartment blocks along the ocean were, but it was popular because of its central location and its water views.

Mrs. Miller's apartment on the third floor had only two bedroom suites but a very large living room overlooking the ocean. When Jim was alive, they had sometimes talked about getting a bigger place but now Molly was glad that she had stayed here: it was just big enough for her and an occasional house guest. The Millers had never subscribed to any newfangled ideas of the modern or minimalist school of decorating. They liked a warm, comfortable home with many rugs, pictures and squashy armchairs. Unchanged since Jim's death, it was full of heirlooms, souvenirs, family photographs, embroidered cushions and knickknacks given to them over the years and faithfully kept. No horizontal surfaces, neither tables, nor chests, nor shelves, remained unadorned. Molly had always found it difficult to throw any ornamental or sentimental objects away. Her husband, during his lifetime, had kept her hoarding instincts somewhat under control, but since his death, Molly had given free rein to her accumulative tendencies. Although most items were of little monetary value, they composed a tableau of a certain opulent charm that was a reflection of the owner's body and soul.

Maintaining such a household was labor-intensive. All of the bibelots needed cleaning and dusting, silver had to be polished, glassware kept sparkling, flowers replaced, rugs vacuumed, cushions plumped, and as Molly was house-proud, but disinclined to embark on these tasks herself, a housekeeper had to be engaged. Thus the indispensable Manolita had come into their lives and had now been in charge of all these tasks for many years.

Manolita was Cuban, and proud of it. With her wild black-grey hair and a moustache that many adolescent young men would be proud to have, she was unmistakably Latina. Had there still lingered any doubts, they would have been dispersed the moment she opened her mouth. Despite having lived in Florida for some forty years, her English was still so heavily accented that casual listeners took it to be Spanish until they recognized by chance a few English words. Once you had tuned into Manolita's method and pattern of speech it was possible to have a conversation with her – just.

Molly was completely used to her and besides had decided long time ago that her housekeeper had plenty of sterling qualities to make up for any linguistic defects. She was a hard worker, a divine cook and a woman of sound opinions which she liked to share with her employer, whether encouraged to do so or not. Mrs. Miller, for her part, was very fond of Manolita because she was totally dependable and trustworthy and one of the few people she could share her memories of her late husband with, time and time again.

There was only one stumbling block for their otherwise almost complete domestic harmony: Manolita smoked. She was not just one to enjoy an occasional cigarette, perhaps on the balcony or when she took a well-deserved break. Manolita smoked with total dedication and gusto. Cigarettes were to her as indispensable as bread and water to the hungry and thirsty. What grieved Molly particularly was an aesthetic problem that derived from this unfettered passion. At all times the housekeeper had a cigarette dangling in a corner of her mouth and she could neither be cajoled nor threatened to remove it, even for the occasions when guests came to see Mrs. Miller. Since she insisted on rolling her own brand there was also the issue of the surplus bits of tobacco that were being discarded regularly. Brown specks settled on Manolita's otherwise snowy white apron and, worse than that, she spat them out or extracted them by finger from her lips. Molly, who was a lady, from the top of her glossy curls to the tip of her polished shoes, could never quite come to terms with the uncouth habits of her maid, but if she wanted to continue enjoying Manolita's domestic care, and eating her mouth-watering Cuban cuisine, she had to accept her as she was, tobacco and all.

Today Molly could hardly wait to come home. She knew that the maids in the building loved gossip, and she hoped that for once she could provide Manolita with exciting news before any of her friends found out. Yesterday, Manolita had already left by the time she returned home, and as she always came late to work on Saturdays, Molly had missed her this morning as well. Quite surprisingly, nothing had appeared in the papers so far about the murder. It seemed that highest quarters had managed to muzzle the press for the moment.

With great anticipation Mrs. Miller went straight to the kitchen. "Manolita, you will never believe what happened yesterday morning at the club," she started.

"Como, Senora! They say el senor Robertson, the one who live in that big house, he's dead, no? Chop, chop, hit over the head. Poor Senor! Dios mio! que horror!"

"How did you know, Manolita? It only happened twenty-four hours ago, and there was nothing in the papers or on tv." Mrs. Miller was rather disappointed that her so-called news turned out to be old hat.

"Oh, simple. My friend Lourdes work on the second floor for Senora Forsyth, she hear it from the janitor, who talk to the porter, who has a nephew who work at the club... what you call a caddie."

"Since you are so well informed, Manolita, you don't by any chance know the identity of the murderer," Mrs. Miller wanted to know.

Manolita took a deep drag of her cigarette, where ashes had reached the usual nerve-racking length. Mrs. Miller's eyes were glued to the tip. "No, is too early to say. But that Senor Robertson, he's not very nice gentleman, muy mala gente. Big house, big parties, big money. But very mean man. The uncle of my friend's cousin from Mexico, he work for him once in the garden. He no have no greengcard but very hard worker... Mr. Robertson he tell the butler, if they no have no greengcard, he no have to pay them! 'Let them call the police if they don't like it' he say.... He want to rob them Senora... es un robo! The Frenchman, he pay the worker from his own pocket... and tell him not to come back."

"Oh really? That is quite shocking." Mrs. Miller shook her head. "I don't know the family that well. His wife was charming and the children seem friendly enough."

"Como, Senora, how do you think those rich people get so rich if they not steal it from little people?! My friend's cousin's uncle say Senor Robertson, always very strict with his children too. Last year he go to Mexico, many weeks, two times, three times, they say he have a girlfriend in Mexico."

"Oh Manolita, shush, that is pure gossip. Why should the poor man, being a widower, not travel and perhaps take an interest in a woman? I can't blame him for that. I find it more distressing that someone who is generous to a fault with his friends should be unjustifiably mean with the people who work for him.

"By the way, Manolita, has anyone called?"

"The telephone ring, maybe you have message on the machine," came the answer. Mrs. Miller was quite relieved that Manolita rarely took her calls, as her consequent messages were usually too obscure to be of any use.

Special Agent in Charge Gonzalez' voice was on the answering machine. He introduced himself and proposed to come and see Mrs. Miller at four o'clock unless she called him to cancel the appointment.

A look at her watch confirmed that there was plenty of time to prepare for his visit. "Manolita, please get some tea ready and any biscuits we have. I'll just wash my hands. We are expecting a guest at four."

CHAPTER 6

The doorman rang punctually at four o'clock to announce Agent Gonzalez. Manolita sized him up at the door, and ushered the special agent in. Mrs. Miller greeted him and offered him tea which he gladly accepted. He lowered himself gingerly into an overstuffed pink armchair that matched his tie, and folded his long legs away. Then, once again, he started by explaining the reasons for his involvement in the murder case.

Manolita appeared with Molly's charming English tea set, delicate flower-painted Limoges china, and poured Earl Grey tea, all the while watching Gonzalez to make sure that he didn't steal a teaspoon, for which she might be blamed.

"I am very pleased to meet you, Mrs. Miller, and glad that you could see me at such short notice." Gonzalez looked as happy as a man can, whose features have been settled for years into woeful folds.

"I am very interested in your observations and, to be honest, in your opinions. You have, if I may say so, a certain reputation..." He saw Molly's raised eyebrows and added hastily, "...as a detective, Palm Beach's answer to Miss Marple." He allowed himself a weak smile.

"I am told that you helped the police substantially in solving a rather tricky case of theft two years ago."

Miss Miller blushed most becomingly. "You are too kind, Special Agent. Yes, a young actress lost her extremely valuable engagement ring and she wanted no publicity because she was afraid to upset her fiancé, a film producer with a fearsome temper."

She chuckled at the memory of those exciting days. "I was very happy to give your colleagues a tip here and there. Believe me, it's not as if the police had been negligent but I know this place so well and take such an interest in people. By pure chance I had just made the acquaintance of the young woman and she told me a lot about her life and her circumstances. You see, nobody minds talking to an old lady..."

With a graceful movement of her hand she dismissed his courteous protest. "Anyway, you flatter me with your description. But if there is anything I can do to help, I will happily assist you in any way I can."

"Thank you. I know that you have already given a statement to the Palm Beach detective. However, in view of its importance, and for reasons that I'm not at liberty to discuss, the case has been turned over to us at West Palm Beach satellite office of the Bureau. The murder of Mr. Robertson is very perplexing, very perplexing indeed." He stroked his moustache thoughtfully.

"I think we can rule out the possibility that a stranger came onto the golf course to kill and rob. After all, nothing was taken as far as we know and an expensive watch was still on his wrist. We believe that the murder was committed for other reasons and by someone in Mr. Robertson's circle, at least an acquaintance of his. Would you agree?"

"Why, certainly, Agent Gonzalez" Mrs. Miller nodded with conviction. "Frank's habits, well, the predictability of his movements made it very easy for the murderer. Quite a few people would know about his morning routine. —Please, have some ginger biscuits!"

"So I understand," confirmed Gonzalez. "This is what the golf pro told me: Mr. Robinson played virtually every morning, always from 8:05 a.m. until 8:55 a.m., and always the same number of holes. He started with 10, 11, 12 and 13, which, I understand follow each other. Then, instead of going East to the 14th hole, he crossed over to the right, back past the 10th green to play the 18th hole, and finished the game. This is why Mr. Harvey, after having played the 10th, could see the body, well, first the bag."

"Tell me, Agent Gonzalez," asked Mrs. Miller, "what did the medical examiner have to say about the time of death?"

"I am afraid, Mrs. Miller, that is not very helpful. We know from our witnesses, that the murder must have taken place between 8:35 a.m. and 9:05 a.m., and that tallies with the medical findings, except that in theory death could have occurred half an hour earlier or later."

"I see. Well, how can I help you?" Mrs. Miller wanted to know.

"You have lived here in the neighborhood the longest and, if you don't mind my saying so, you are credited with very good powers of observation. I would be particularly grateful if you could fill me in on some of the people who live here. Leaving his immediate household apart, can you think of anyone who might have had a motive to kill Mr. Robertson? Did he have any enemies, as far as you know?"

"Dear, oh dear, enemies? I don't know, Agent Gonzalez. I think I can say without being indiscreet that Frank was not the most diplomatic of men, a little rough and too direct, if you know what I mean. There certainly were tensions between him and Frederick Brownlow, the Evergreen Club president. It's not that they clashed publicly, but you just felt they were rather uncomfortable in each other's company. If I recall correctly, a certain animosity existed right from the start, when the Robertsons moved to Palm Beach, well over twenty years ago, maybe even thirty... time passes so quickly," Molly mused.

After a moment she carried on: "I don't know whether they had met previously or whether they just hit it off badly from the start. You could speak to Brownlow about it, but I doubt that you will get anything out of him. He is a gentleman, of course, and can be charming if he chooses. He certainly is always very kind to me and went out of his way to show his sympathy when my dear husband Jim died. Well, let me put it this way: being on terms of less than perfect harmony with some of the people around you hardly makes you a candidate to murder - or to be murdered."

"I agree, Mrs. Miller. Let's carry on. How about Robertson's other friends? Tell me what you know."

"Well, Francis had golf partners occasionally, of course, but I think he really preferred to play by himself. If he had close friends, I would not know about them. I think, he didn't know how to make friends and did not seem to care, as long as he was respected. He entertained generously, but not anyone in particular, just casual friends, members of the golf club etc. As you probably know, his wife died some years ago. She was a lovely lady and there were no scandals. To the best of my knowledge, he never had any subsequent serious relationships with other women which, now that I think about it, is rather strange. After all he is not old, at least for Palm Beach, and he is still a handsome man... I mean, he was a handsome man. Oh dear!"

"The children are charming. How well he gets on with them, I have no idea. I have never heard of any serious falling out between them, although I can imagine that he was quite a demanding and domineering father. His daughter is married to a very pleasant man from Pittsburgh. They have one boy. The son, Sam, lives in New York. He is unmarried. There was always a rumor that linked him with Marylou Baker. She is a very clever girl with an art gallery on Via Parigi. Her mother is a friend of mine, Birdie Baker, so lovely, and still very attractive."

"Have you met the deceased's brother-in-law, Mr. Fellows? He is apparently staying at the house with a girl-friend," Gonzalez wanted to know.

"Oh, really? My, my, that is good to hear. I am surprised, though, because the two men got on all right when his wife Elizabeth was alive, but when she died they had an argument. I can't remember who told me that, or what it was about. Anyway, since then Gillian has rarely been here in Palm Beach. You have met him?"

When the agent nodded, she carried on. "Gil is handsome and charming, a writer as far as I know. I couldn't say whether he is any good or successful. You'll have to ask him."

"I will. Then there are Mr. and Mrs. Harris. They were at the house, when Mr. Robertson died. What do you know about them?"

"Well, yes, I guess you could call Peggy and Martin his friends," conceded Mrs. Miller. "Peggy was close to the late Mrs. Robertson. They have no family. Martin is some sort of contractor, he has a building company, and they live on Middle Road. I don't think they are members of the Evergreen Club, but they are very much 'old Palm Beach'."

She stopped for a moment and looked at Gonzalez, who had been making some notes.

"What about the neighbors on Golfview Road?" he wanted to know.

"Well, they are all very quiet and respectable. You no doubt met Osbert Harvey, who lives in the big house with his mother. He is a delightful man, the life and soul of every party. A little under the thumb of his mother, but such a devoted son!

"And then there is Henry Standing, a widower. Have you met him?" Gonzalez nodded again, and although he remembered it as a pleasant encounter, his face remained habitually morose.

"I think he was on quite friendly terms with Frank. But then, Henry is on friendly terms with everybody. A delightful man, don't you think?" Mrs. Miller blushed a little. "We are quite good friends and occasionally we go on little outings in one of his vintage cars. Such a lark!" She smiled. Henry Standing clearly stirred some tender feelings in her.

"Then there are the two domestic employees. The butler, I can never remember his name, a French gentleman, and the housekeeper, Marjorie. They have both been with the Robertsons for quite a few years."

Molly stopped for a moment and then added: "I imagine we have to ask ourselves: who would benefit from Frank's death?"

"Thank you, Mrs. Miller. That largely confirms what we already know. Yes, who benefits? We heard from Robertson's attorney that his considerable fortune goes to his children with a number of legacies: to his university, a few charities, and there are two, not inconsiderable sums set aside for the butler and the housekeeper.

"To some small extent one could attach a motive to everybody. We found out that Mr. Wallace, his son-in-law, is far from wealthy. In fact he is strapped for money and has some serious debts. How aware of this Mrs. Wallace is, I have no idea. By the way, what do you think of the boy? I found him very sullen and evasive, sort of shifty and monosyllabic. A typical teenager, I guess, but I wondered whether he uses drugs, as so many young people do these days. His mother seems quite concerned about him.

"The Harris's seem to live on a very comfortable scale, but they too are in debt. I discovered that Mr. Harris made quite a lot of money ten years ago, but has had no major, and certainly no regular income since then. Someone mentioned that he might want to get his hands on the Robertson's house, which would be easier now, after the old gentleman's death."

They remained silent for a moment. Gonzalez continued down his mental list. "Marylou Baker is certainly an engaging young woman. But I would have thought a small gallery with such low turnover is less than fulfilling for a woman of her education and energy. Her life would improve dramatically if her close friend, Sam Robertson, inherited a fortune, moved to Palm Beach, and perhaps helped her put the gallery on a different scale and maybe even married her!"

After a short pause the well-informed special agent in charge continued gloomily. "A murder inquiry looks into motive and opportunity. You see, leaving the motive aside, we have a bit of a problem with opportunity. The events yesterday morning happened as follows, and this is well documented through reliable witnesses: Mr. Robertson left the house as always at eight o'clock with his golf bag. He wore his usual beige trousers, a polo shirt and his navy golfer's cap. He started his game at 8:05 a.m. The last person to see him alive was Mr. Standing, to whom he waved, as was his habit, after teeing off for the 13th hole. Mr. Standing had a very clear view from his dressing room over that part of the golf course.

"He said that he saw Robertson hit the ball and walk towards the green. Mr. Standing is absolutely certain about this. He checked his watch because it amuses him that his friend and neighbor is such a creature of habit. The time was just after 8:35

a.m. The body was found at 9:07 a.m. by Mr. Harvey. So, you see the murder was committed between, let's say 8:36 a.m. and 8:55 a.m., because by then Mr. Robertson would normally have finished his game and returned to his house.

"Now, all the people in Mr. Robertson's circle have a perfect alibi for these nineteen minutes." Gonzalez shifted his weight in the pink chair and continued. "His family, as well as the two domestics were in the house, respectively in the garden, except for Gillian Fellows who was out running. Marylou Baker was seen leaving her gallery at 8:40 a.m. Mr. and Mrs. Harris were spotted by neighbors, and their gardener saw them as well. Mr. Harvey was with his mother and the nurse at the time in question and did not get to the golf course until nine. Mr. Brownlow is the person with the easiest access to the murder scene, as his garden is immediately adjoining the course. His residence is the only one that is not separated by the road like his neighbors, but he telephoned his secretary at 8:30 a.m. and never left his house after that, making and accepting phone calls continuously.

"What do you know about the butler and the housekeeper, Mrs. Miller?"

"Very little, I am afraid," she answered. "I think Marjorie may have had designs on Frank when she first took up her post. Mind you, she was quite an attractive woman then, and a few years younger. Whether they actually ever had an affair, once Frank was a free man, I have no idea. I guess it is not impossible. I've always had the feeling she is a woman "on the make". If she dreamed of becoming the second Mrs. Robertson, she must have been very disappointed. Unrequited love or, to put it more harshly, dissatisfied greed, could certainly be a motive for ill will, I don't know about murder.

"And the butler?" she went on. "I think that despite his best efforts, he always looks somewhat raffish... 'but of course, ee is French,'" said Molly, mocking his accent. "There were rumors that he's a gambling and a betting man, rather more than is prudent. I am afraid my source is perhaps not completely trustworthy. I have it on the authority of my maid – you met Manolita just now. She has not actually seen this for herself, but she heard from a relation who is a friend of a friend, that the butler is regularly seen at the dog races, and sometimes on the "Sea Princess", the gaming boat that operates outside Palm Beach waters, and it's said that he has lost large amounts of money on occasion."

After a moment's deliberation, Mrs. Miller looked at her visitor. "If you don't mind, Special Agent Gonzalez, let's discuss the actual assault. Am I right in thinking that poor Frank was attacked with one of his own golf clubs which, doubtless, shows no finger prints other than his own?"

"Correct, Mrs. Miller. He was hit with considerable force several times on the head. The first blow would have stunned him instantly, and any of the following three or four blows could have killed him. A sand wedge is a powerful weapon."

"Of course, you realize, don't you, that Frank must have known his killer," said Molly.

"How so?" enquired Gonzalez, genuinely surprised. "Why do you say that?"

"Do I understand correctly that Frank was bludgeoned to death with his own iron? Look, a stranger would not have been able to get to Frank's golf bag and extract a club without a loud argument, probably some shouting and then a fight. But nothing was heard, and there were no signs of a fight. That leaves me to conclude, that the victim knew his killer. Mr. X, who was known to Frank, showed up on the course, they talked and when Frank turned his back to him he pulled out the club and struck him. In other words, the murderer was probably acquainted with the victim, most likely a fellow golfer, although not necessarily so, as quite a few people walk on the course without being there to play golf."

They sat for a moment in silence, the agent stroking his moustache thoughtfully. Then Mrs. Miller continued: "And there is another thing, Mr. Gonzalez. You know, that it is not impossible to gain access to the course, I mean even for non-members. I've often noticed that there are small openings in the hedge and fence surrounding the golf course in a few places, on Golfview Road as well as around the corner, on South County Road. That means, virtually anybody could have approached Frank Robertson."

"Yes, indeed, that has occurred to us. I must say, Mrs. Miller, you live up to your reputation as a super sleuth." He allowed himself a sad little smile. "So, we probably need to widen the circle of suspects. At present we have no idea who did it. If you have any other recollections, Mrs. Miller, or if you can think of any little details that might help us, please get in touch with me." With these words, Gonzalez got up, thanked his hostess for the tea and biscuits and left her.

Mrs. Miller could not suppress a little smile of pleasurable anticipation. It had been an exciting time, when the actress' ring had gone missing and was finally found, with her help. And now something similar seemed to have developed - another mystery - and again she was in the middle of it. How very considerate of the Special Agent in Charge to have asked for her help. He seemed to be a lovely man, maybe a little sad, and she was not sure that she totally approved of his taste in clothes. His shirt, with its lilac hue, however faint, had alarmed her a little. It would never have been permitted near her Jim's closet, but then, Gonzales was Latin, he was younger and fashions changed. If they were going to work together on this case, and it looked as though they might, she would have ample opportunity to find out whether this was just a deplorable one-off aberration, as she saw it, or an inkling of future unorthodox sartorial choices.

CHAPTER 7

SUNDAY

At seven o'clock Mrs. Miller emerged from her leisurely bath, smelling faintly of violets. She was dressed in a light cotton kimono printed with a cheerful paisley pattern. With a contented sigh, she mixed herself a weak martini. Life was not too bad, really. Of course it would never again be what it was with dear Jim but as long as she had her health and her dear friends around her, as long as she could afford her present life style, she had nothing to complain about.

Too sad, what happened to poor Francis! If only she could help the 'special agent in charge'... (she loved his title). He seemed to be a nice enough man, patient, polite and at least eager to listen. The problem was that he was coming in as an 'outsider' to Palm Beach and this group of people. It certainly was clever of him to realize this, and to ask for her help.

Her thoughts turned to the guest she was expecting: Lucy de Silva. Poor Lucy, how bravely she dealt with her affliction. She was so glad to be able to show her old friend some kindness and hospitality. They had been to church together earlier. Molly was a regular at The Poinciana Chapel on Coconut Row. She was well aware that many of her friends considered the romantic-looking, neo-gothic Bethesda-by-the-Sea to be socially superior, but the Millers had always felt more at home in the nondenominational Chapel, a simple white clapboard building with gardens running down to the lake. They loved the plain interior with its huge, arched Georgian windows that flooded the church with light.

After refreshments in the Fellowship Hall, the ladies had enjoyed an excellent lunch at Testa's (Molly adored their eggs Benedict). Although the distance between the church and the restaurant was negligible, Molly had insisted on using the car – for Lucy's benefit. It had been a wholly satisfactory outing, only slightly marred on their way back, when Lucy pointed to a bare plot of land on the corner of South Ocean Boulevard and Seaspray Avenue and wanted to know why it was empty.

Mrs. Miller had brought the car to an abrupt halt and turned to her friend. "Oh my dear, you have no idea what happened here. I'll tell you and it's not a pretty story. Just thinking back on it makes me so angry. It started, what, about four years ago; yes I think in the spring of 2001. Two enterprising businessmen purchased one of Mizner's last masterpieces, the aptly named Casa Encantada in Manalapan. This is an area just a few miles south of Palm Beach. Having also bought this beautiful piece of land, they lifted the mansion in sections from its foundations, shipped it over on barges and placed it here on the ground. The plan was to renovate the house and sell it at an enormous profit. So far, so good. All this attracted huge attention, people were gathered here all the time, and the Shiny Sheet ran daily articles. Then the drama turned into comedy and finally tragedy. The partners fell out. The town hall authorities gave them a deadline to put the house on proper foundations, before the hurricane season. Time, and presumably money, ran out and guess what? This lovely, historically significant building was pulled down—reduced to rubble and carted off. Preservationists and architectural aficionados were up in arms, but also a lot of ordinary people, like me, were horrified that this could happen in our enlightened times. I am afraid this little story illustrates some of the strengths and weaknesses of this place: great enterprise, imagination, huge investments—but also short sightedness and greed."

Lucy shook her head sadly and took a last look at the vacant lot. Molly started the car again. "I am sorry, if I sound like one of those 'hysterical preservationists', (that's what the real estate developers call us), but I am horrified by such events. Well, after this little sermon I better take you home." The ladies had agreed to have a rest before meeting again later in the evening, and Lucy was now due to arrive any minute.

"I just hope she likes Manolita's Cuban chicken dish," Molly thought to herself. But why wouldn't she? Everybody enjoyed this delicious concoction of chicken breast, onion, tomatoes, pepper and peas, in a delicately flavored sauce. She suddenly wondered if Manolita had remembered to leave some cooked rice and dessert before she went home. She was about to open a bottle of wine, when right on cue, the house telephone rang and the doorman announced her visitor.

Lucy, yet again, had made her way to her friend's house on foot with the help of her crutches. The ladies sat down and Molly triumphantly lifted up a substantial leather tome. "Look, Lucy, I found an old photograph album with pictures of all of us. You'll love this. Do you need glasses?" she wanted to know.

"No thank you, Molly. My eyesight is still perfect. I am so lucky. Let me see, how exciting that you found this book." The ladies bent over the volume in eager anticipation.

After some ten minutes Molly looked up. "I am hungry, let's get something to eat. My maid cooked my favorite dish for us. I just need to warm it up. You stay here and look at the album, it will all be ready in a few minutes."

With these words Molly disappeared into her little kitchen. Lucy was listening to the clatter of dishes and doors, when the lights suddenly went out. They were not in pitch dark, as Molly always lit some candles in the evening and this she had done tonight as well. She called out from the kitchen: "Lucy, darling, I am so sorry. I have dirty hands, could you just do me a favor? Look in front of you by the front door. There is a little cupboard in the corner. Just flip the circuit breaker, then we'll have light again. But don't touch the 220!"

From the kitchen Molly heard Lucy get up and make her way to the little panel box by the entrance. Then her friend called out: "Which switch is it?"

"It's the smaller one, the 120. Can you see it?"

"Yes, ok," Lucy called back and instantly the light returned.

By now Mrs. Miller had cleaned her hands and rejoined her friend. "Sorry about that," she explained. "The building was not planned for the amount of electricity one needs these days, and we have become quite used to the occasional blackout. Now we're all right. I hope you'll drink a glass of white wine?" Lucy nodded and the ladies sat down to a much praised meal.

Inevitably their thoughts returned to their childhood and school days. "You know, Lucy, I never met your brother-in-law, Lily's husband. What was he like? How long were they married?... and tell me about their daughter!"

"All right." Lucy smiled. "One question at a time! As you remember, Lily was five years younger than we are. She trained as an actress and she was even quite successful. I saw her on the stage a few times and in some small parts on television. Simon, the man she eventually married, was a colleague. They met when she was in her thirties, on stage, as it were. He was a few years older. They appeared together, somewhere in the provinces, in a Noel Coward play: Private Lives, I believe. They tried to find work together, which was difficult. Then he turned to directing and did rather well.

"Eventually she had her daughter Gail, and took a break from her acting career. I didn't see much of them in those days, because they had moved to San Francisco. We were all shocked when they split up. I think he had rather a lot of affairs and after a while she couldn't take it any more. He moved around, wherever he could find work. Lily remained in San Francisco and made a living working in theater administration and promotion. The little girl was adorable. I saw her once or twice every year. Simon drifted out of their lives. I understand he traveled all over the world; he may be dead by now, for all I know.

"Five years ago my sister died in a car crash. At the time her daughter, Gail, was going to art school to study painting. She was a beautiful girl, very sweet, rather romantic. She definitely had talent but she was always highly strung and somewhat restless. Some time after her mother's death she moved to Mexico, to an artist's colony in San Miguel de Allende. She loved the light, she said, and did some extraordinary work. They experimented with different media and styles and, it has to be said, also with drugs. At first Gail just wanted to stimulate her imagination and used some relatively harmless recreational drugs. Then she started taking more, stronger stuff, and more frequently. She was emotionally quite fragile. She had always been very excitable and impressionable. Anyway, she had some problems, a love affair, her work was not going well and then..."

Lucy stopped. She was clearly upset and could not carry on. Molly quickly got up and put her arm around her friend. "Shush, my dear. Don't talk about it. It must be so painful for you. Just remember, she's at peace now. She's in a better world. Let me get you a glass of water. I'm so sorry. I should never have asked you. Did you see your niece in those days, when she lived in San Miguel?"

Lucy made a brave effort to pull herself together. She drank some of the water and managed to continue. "No. I have never been to Mexico. I always wanted to go, but I left it too late..."

"What a tragedy, that such a beautiful, young life ended so prematurely," said Molly. "But I am sure there was nothing you and Lily could have done. We have to accept it as God's will. As you know, I never had children, which is also very sad. You and your sister had this wonderful gift of a beautiful young woman in your lives and then you lost it. I don't know which is worse. Life can be so very sad and it's good that we don't know what the future has in store for us."

CHAPTER 8

MONDAY

Marjorie Pitts whispered into the telephone, clearly agitated. "You know I don't want you to call me during working hours... What do you mean 'emergency'? Listen... listen...! Tim... Darling...! I've heard that before, 'unexpected expenses'. Why do you have to immediately spend every penny I give you?" She hissed now. "No, not today. No, that's impossible. Please, I can't talk right now. I'll call you later." She hung up. Maurice, who stood hidden from sight on the other side of the open double doors, hardly dared to breathe as he remained motionless until the woman's steps faded away.

* * *

Another perfect day in paradise and Birdie was on her way to collect Marylou from her gallery for lunch. Leaving her apartment building she walked along Brazilian Avenue, past the enchanting gardens of one of the island's best loved hotels, the Brazilian Court which had its main entrance on the other side of the block, on Australian Avenue.

The Brazilian Court consisted of low stucco buildings, surrounding two courtyards. Recently it had been extensively — and expensively — renovated, and its eatery, Café Boulud, had become a huge success. This flower-filled oasis of luxurious splendor was once the setting of a tragic event, yet again involving the Kennedy family.

In April 1984 the clan had gathered in Palm Beach to celebrate the matriarch Rose Kennedy's birthday. Old Joe Kennedy, who in the twenties had chased Gloria Swanson all over Palm Beach, was dead by then, as were his sons, Jack and Robert. David, twenty-eight years old, the third son of Robert and Ethel Kennedy, had been put up at the Brazilian Court Hotel, as the mansion was too small to accommodate the whole, extended family. David was a troubled young man with a history of drug and alcohol abuse and in Palm Beach it was no different. He spent the weekend socializing and drinking, looking for and taking drugs. On the morning of the 25th he was expected to check out of the hotel. His mother became alarmed when he failed to turn up at Boston Airport. She rang the Kennedy compound and Caroline, David's cousin, raced to the hotel. There was no answer when she knocked at the door of room 107 and called his name. She left without entering his room. A short while later Ethel Kennedy called the hotel concierge and asked him to check the room. They found David Kennedy dead. A few hours earlier he had injected himself with a highly dangerous drug cocktail that killed him instantly.

Birdie shuddered involuntarily every time she remembered those events, but today her mind was on other, more pleasant things. She was looking forward to spending some time – and sharing a good meal – with her daughter in one of their favorite restaurants.

When she arrived at the gallery in Via Parigi, Marylou was waiting for her. Together they strolled through some of the other Vias before emerging onto Worth Avenue.

Perhaps the greatest jewel in Mizner's crown, more so than the Evergreen Club, El Mirasol and countless other grand buildings, were these charming little shopping arcades he designed to house his workshops and his offices. In Via Mizner he built himself a five-story tower house, and later he constructed a similar one for his friend, in a lane called Via Parigi (after Paris Singer complained that the architect had "his own" Via, but that he, the patron, did not). The Vias were meant to resemble romantic Mediterranean villages and they do, except that they are cleaner, better kept and more picturesque than any place you could find in Italy, Spain, or Southern France.

Unlike the club, which is only open to its lucky few members and their guests, the Vias are open to everyone. They consist of delicately scaled and delightfully varied buildings, arcades, plazas and walkways containing shops, apartments, galleries and restaurants. No two houses are the same. What serious architectural critics might put down to pastiche, is really a highly successful, delicious little Mediterranean "folly" in sorbet colors, with tiled roofs, ornamental balconies and loggias, fountains and gardens. The materials Mizner chose were painted stucco, massive wrought iron, hand-formed terra cotta barrel tiles and pecky Cyprus wood. Rumor goes that these "hand made" roof tiles were actually formed over the thighs of burly workmen and then fired.

As Mizner hated anything that looked new, he went to extraordinary lengths to make his buildings appear timeworn. In his factories, tiles were attacked with a hammer and the broken pieces cemented back into place. He poured corrosive chemicals on walls and floors and had workmen scrub them with steel brushes. Furniture was riddled with buckshot to imitate the devastation of the wood worm or beaten with iron chains to age them. Cypress wood was bashed and hacked to resemble true pecky cypress, which results from a fungal attack.

Mother and daughter walked down Worth Avenue, Florida's answer to Rodeo Drive and Bond Street. Limousines rolled noiselessly past them, the staccato of high heels echoed against the plate glass windows of Tiffany and Ralph Lauren, Chanel and Cartier. Lunch time was Worth Avenue's finest hour, when it became a catwalk of eternal youth. Determination was written large on the flawless faces of ladies who shopped until ready to drop. Their cupboards were full to bursting, but there was always room for another cute hat, a new, desirable piece of jewelry. Festooned with carrier bags, they finally retreated to the Evergreen Club or Ta-boo, Renato's or Bice, to consider the damage done so far and decide on further battle plans.

Marylou and Birdie were heading for one of Palm Beach's best-loved restaurants, Ta-boo, located on Worth Avenue and stretching all the way through the whole block to Peruvian Avenue. Since 1941 it had catered during its long, eventful existence to generations of Palm Beach families as well as celebrities like the Windsors, the Kennedys, Gary Cooper, Frank Sinatra and Richard Nixon.

Once inside the narrow entrance, the room extended back far beyond the long bar on the left and widened into further sections on both sides. The whole place was rather dark, womb-like, and cozy. The decor incorporated everything Palm Beach loved: rattan and bamboo furniture, leopard printed rugs and fabrics, monkey designs, trellis work and a jungle of plants.

The food was always good and not particularly expensive, the staff superbly attentive—no wonder, as more often than not the owner, the urbane Franklyn DeMarco, was in attendance to greet his customers who frequently were his friends. Ta-boo was a popular meeting place, day and night, early and late, for men and women, lovers, friends and married couples. When Birdie and Marylou arrived, Franklyn was on hand to greet them affectionately as regulars and take them to their table on the fashionable left side of the back room. Birdie looked around with satisfaction: nothing had changed here for years. Redecoration and updates were so skillfully engineered that, work completed, an area looked refreshed but never jarringly new. She used to dine here regularly with her late husband. Later she carried on a few light-hearted flirtations within these same four walls.

Birdie was aware that quite a few heads turned as she walked through the room. In this subdued light, with her lovely figure and perfect posture, she could easily be taken for a "girl" in her thirties. An old adage could have been coined for her and in fact it had become one of her eagerly repeated mantras: "A woman should look like a girl but act like a lady."

Today she had chosen to wear Steven Stolman linen trousers with a large flowery print in blues and greens, combined with a crisp white shirt, a green cable-knit sweater casually draped around her shoulders, a bag in the same green, and open sandals displaying immaculately pedicured toes. She knew she looked just right and felt quiet satisfaction.

Opening the menu, Birdie gave her daughter a critical look. With a subdued sigh she took in the usual sober picture Marylou presented. Where others saw an attractive young woman, with her discreet appearance conveying a strong sense of personality, her mother only registered that her daughter's black trousers were somewhat shapeless, her shirt nondescript, and her shoes sturdy rather than dainty. Unlike her mother, there was nothing playful and expressly feminine about Marylou.

Mother and daughter asked for water and discussed the food on offer. Both decided on *paillard de saumon*, and iced tea.

As they had not seen each other for a couple of days, there was much to discuss, not the least of which was the recent bloodshed in their midst.

"Darling, do you have any idea when the funeral will take place? There were those long articles in the papers about poor Francis, but nothing was mentioned about that!" was Birdie's first question.

"Yes, it happened actually yesterday, but it was done very quietly. Due to the circumstances, nobody was invited. Only the immediate family was present," answered Marylou.

"I hated some of the stuff I read in the papers," continued her mother. "Journalists can be a pain. Even in these sad circumstances they cannot pass up the chance to make a pun. Did you see that: 'The golf CLUB murder?' Please!!!" She gave a deep sigh. "I can't wait for the whole thing to be over. Do you know if the police have made an arrest yet, or if they have any clues at least? You must have seen Sam recently. Did he tell you anything?" Birdie wanted to know.

"Yes, of course I have seen him, but as far as he knows, the police are still in the dark. They certainly haven't arrested anyone. Of course they keep questioning everybody in Sam's family, including the butler and the housekeeper, but it seems, everybody has an alibi for the time of the murder. Oh, by the way, do you also feel that Maurice, the butler, is a rather strange character? The way he always glides so noiselessly around the place, popping up behind you unexpectedly… I don't know… he is certainly efficient, but also slightly disturbing. Anyway, it seems he comes alive off duty. Apparently he is a well-known and inveterate gambler, betting like mad at the dog track and on the 'Sea Princess'".

When her mother nodded, she continued: "Of course, none of that is a crime, but it amuses me. It just goes to show how little you can judge people by their appearance."

"Very true," agreed Birdie with a meaningful look at her daughter's plain and clearly well-worn cardigan. "What about the housekeeper? Have any sinister secrets come to light about her?"

"Well, believe it or not," exclaimed Marylou triumphantly, "they have! Maurice told the FBI agent, who's conducting the enquiry, that he suspects Marjorie of having a young lover. It seems he overheard some phone calls or such and he felt it was his moral duty – as he calls it – to tell the police, and no doubt they will find out if there is any truth to what, at present, is just a rumor. All it means is that Marjorie might have been in need of money—just possibly like Maurice."

"Fascinating," mumbled her mother. "By the way, talking about money: do you still need that loan from me? I have talked to my bank manager and he said he could let me have $50,000, if you really need it for your business."

"Oh Mother, you are an angel. I should never have mentioned it. That was just an idea - to buy more stock - in an attempt to increase my turn over, and hopefully make a bigger profit. I have the most wonderful news for you, which I wanted to tell you right away: Sam offered to become my partner in the gallery! He wants to give it a major cash injection and even talked about renting larger premises. He definitely will get involved personally and wants to work with me. I had always hoped he would come back to live in Palm Beach and that's exactly what he is planning to do. He has to return to New York for a while, but when he comes back it will be for good."

Marylou could not suppress a big, happy smile that made her eyes sparkle and brought a glow to her face. Having received her mother's wholehearted congratulations on these happy plans for the future, Marylou asked with a twinkle: "Tell me, Mother, what have you been doing with yourself these last few days? Broken any poor bachelor's heart?"

The question was clearly a light-hearted tease, but also a surreptitious test, and Marylou watched her mother cautiously. She would never want to see her hurt and rejected again. Thankfully there was not even a hint of unease in Birdie's reaction.

"Darling," came the mock protest. "Don't say that, even in jest. Your mother is old and crusty and no longer takes any interest in affairs of the heart for herself. I had dinner with dear Osbert yesterday which was quite an experience, but certainly no threat to my virtue. His mother is giving him such a hard time. Yet again, she has initiated an economy drive, which sends the whole household into complete panic. As you know, Aline does not want to forfeit any of her personal comfort, so the only money-saving idea she could come up with, was the exchange of regular light bulbs to those of a lower wattage. As a result, the advent of dusk creates total chaos in the house. We dined practically by candle light only, which is flattering for one's looks, but not terribly safe. Vincent just missed the table with his tray and a whole lot of antique crystal glasses smashed to the floor. The day before, Osbert himself had slipped on the dimly-lit stairs and it is a miracle that he didn't break every bone in his body. But it is worst for the cook: You know that Spanish chef they sometimes employ?"

Marylou shook her head but urged her mother to continue.

"Well. You can hear him swearing in the kitchen. Apparently it is so dark in there that he works with the help of two strong flashlights... Osbert was frightfully embarrassed by it all.

"Aline is sometimes really so unreasonable and even cruel, especially considering how devoted he is to her. Do you remember the lunch he gave for her for her last birthday? He set the table himself, all the decorations were in amethyst, his mother's favorite color and when the ladies unfolded their napkins, each one contained a semiprecious stone. Well, not many sons would do that for their mother.

"But if he wants something, it usually falls on deaf ears. Apparently he asked how she felt about building a swimming pool in the back garden. Do you know what she said? 'Heavens no! Why? We are unlikely to have any little Harveys around the house, are we?'"

"Poor Osbert!"

Marylou could not suppress a smile. She loved hearing about Palm Beach society gossip from her mother. It was racy perhaps, but not vicious, usually full of humor and concern. Through her mother she knew more about what was going on among the older generation than among her contemporaries. She was especially relieved that her mother appeared so at ease. It did not look as if there were any dark clouds on the horizon.

She encouraged her mother to finish the lunch with a little sorbet, then coffee and at three o'clock they parted with a warm embrace.

* * *

"One string? Two strings?" Molly Miller was talking to herself as she came out of Via Parigi and almost collided with her newest friend. "Goodness Gracious me! Agent Gonzalez, I do apologize, sometimes I just don't look where I am going." She looked flustered, but nonetheless charming as usual. A pretty pleated skirt in a small pastel print showed just the right amount of leg for a still attractive woman of her age. A pink twin set, offset by a pearl necklace, completed the pleasing outfit. As this was obviously just a quick shopping trip, not the self-prescribed daily exercise, Molly was wearing low-heeled open-toe pumps rather than the white sneakers. Even Gonzalez, some thirty years her junior, had to admit that she was a fine-looking woman (for her age, he added silently).

"Do you have a minute?" she wanted to know. "We could just sit down and talk for a moment. Let's go into the Via de Lela. There are a couple of benches."

"Excellent idea, Mrs. Miller," agreed Gonzalez without hesitation as he followed her across the road and past the Gucci courtyard and Palm Beach's oldest shop, Kassatly's linen store, into yet another enchanting little green oasis. As they settled companionably on a bench, Molly noticed that the agent pushed his feet as far back as possible as if to hide them. Thus alerted, she took a closer look and could barely conceal a smile. Gonzalez sported a pair of improbable, rather raffish looking two-tone shoes in black and white, and he seemed painfully aware that they were, well, unusual, to say the least. The agent caught her smile, which increased his discomfort. Why, oh why, had he given in that morning to Teresa's demand that he wear these shoes that she had made him buy despite his protest. He was beginning to suspect that her fashion sense might be influenced by the movies she watched. Perhaps an old Valentino film had stirred in her the longing to see her spouse dressed up in these "gigolo" shoes, as Gonzalez called them. This could be a dangerous precedent. If she saw Peter Falk on tv, he might be condemned to wearing an old raincoat in future.

The situation needed delicate handling. Emilio Gonzalez, surrounded in his working life by violence and bloodshed, valued his domestic peace. He considered himself lucky that their discrepancy in matters of taste was really the only stumbling block in an otherwise harmonious relationship, and he was not inclined to jeopardize this for the sake of some extravagant footwear. He forced himself to turn his mind back to the murder inquiry.

114

"Mrs. Miller, there are a few things I wanted to run by you anyway. Did you say anything just now about strings? You haven't by any chance discovered the murderer and have plans to string him up, have you?"

She smiled wanly at his little joke. "I wish I knew! No, no, I just nipped over to one of my favorite shops, Barzina, do you know it?" Without waiting for her companion's expected denial she carried on: "Gretchen, the owner, brings those divine pearls over from China. We are all waiting for the next delivery and I cannot decide whether to opt for one string – modest but becoming – or two strings of pearls – a little more showy but still traditional. You don't have any views on the matter I suppose," she added hopefully.

Gonzalez gravely confirmed that any knowledge of pearls and the reasons for choosing the right number of strings had not ever entered his mental orbit. But he promised to let her know immediately, should he form an opinion on the matter in future.

Mrs. Miller nodded solemnly. She then returned to the murder case. "You know, thinking about our recent conversation brought something back into my mind that I had completely forgotten. Well, it must have been lying dormant in my sub-conscience, as the psychologists would say. Freud was very keen on the sub-conscience, you know. They have now found out that so many of his discoveries that were pooh-poohed, have been confirmed through recent research. This may be so, but there is still a lot that makes no sense to me at all. Take for instance penis envy…"

Noticing the special agent's surprised look, Mrs. Miller blushed and quickly added: "Sorry, this may bore you, but psychology is one of my interests. It comes with the job, as you must know, with this detective work.

"But to return to the case: You asked me about the relationship between Francis and Frederick Brownlow which, as everybody agrees, was a tense one.

"This little incident I am going to tell you about occurred several years ago and at the time it seemed completely unimportant. It is only in the light of recent events that it may have some significance. Anyway, quite a few years ago, I went for a little walk in Pan's garden. Do you know the delightful little public garden on the corner of Hibiscus Avenue and Peruvian Avenue, just behind the splendid new building of the Preservation Foundation?"

Gonzalez shook his head but promised to visit it shortly.

"I passed behind a bench on which two men sat talking – nothing unusual or special in that. But as I was almost out of earshot, I heard them talk in a foreign language. Don't ask me what it was, I am no linguist, but it sounded rather guttural, maybe Swedish or Russian or even German. I turned round and looked a little closer. I recognized Frank and Frederick and saw Frederick handing over an envelope to Frank. Then they got up and went their different ways. They didn't see me and must have thought the place was deserted. Well, that's all. I just remember thinking at the time that it was odd to come across these two men, sitting together on a park bench, when they normally barely exchange the time of day. Do you think you can do something with that bit of information?"

"Thank you, Mrs. Miller. We are just in the process of digging deeper into the past of the murder victim as well as anybody connected with him. As soon as we have found anything, I will let you know.

"By the way, did you know that Mrs. Pitts might have a lover? The butler just put us onto it. It seems he overheard some telephone conversations."

116

"As a matter of fact," said Molly, "I may be able to help you there as well. You must begin to think that I do nothing all day but keep watch over my friends and acquaintances here in Palm Beach. This is not the case, but I do have a lot of time on my hands, and I think I can claim to be a keen observer of human nature. And then, Palm Beach is such a small place that you are constantly thrown together with the same people.

"Just the other day I needed a new daytime outfit for a lunch party at Club Colette... I suppose you are not familiar with Club Colette?" The agent confirmed this with a little sigh.

"Never mind, I made my way to a consignment store in Sunset Avenue that stocks the most darling little Chanel suits. And yes, they had not one, but two that fit me. One was turquoise with the usual braids and buttons, double breasted and a narrow skirt. The other one, in a rust-colored tweed, had a wider skirt with a long slit and a lapel that showed the very pretty lining of the jacket. I'm sorry. This must be boring for you. Anyway, I found it hard to decide and retreated to Green's Pharmacy to think the matter over."

"Were you feeling unwell, Mrs. Miller," asked Gonzalez mechanically.

"Oh no, Green's Pharmacy is also a luncheonette – quite an institution in Palm Beach. Everybody goes there. It's the only completely classless place on the island. Multimillionaires go – the Kennedys all went - and so do all the contractors working here. The food is simple, good and cheap, the waitresses can be quite fierce though. You should try it, Agent Gonzalez! You can't miss it: it's on the corner of North County Road and Sunrise Avenue, with a green and white canopy."

Gonzalez promised to try it, and waited patiently for the continuation of Mrs. Miller's narrative.

"By the time I arrived, just before four, the luncheon area was already closed. When I turned to leave, I noticed a couple sitting at the counter with their back to me, deep in conversation. Something compelled me to look into the mirror in front of them that showed their faces, and I recognized the woman as Marjorie Pitts, Francis' housekeeper. What puzzled me was the fact that she was holding the hand of the young man who sat next to her. They seemed to be on very familiar terms, if you know what I mean, with their heads close together and the way they were talking softly together....not that I heard anything that was spoken." The last remark Mrs. Miller added somewhat regretfully.

"So, that leads us to believe the butler, namely that Mrs. Pitts is conducting an affair and, as you say, with a much younger man. How old do you think he was? Thirty? Forty?"

"That's hard to say, because I only saw their backs and a little of their faces. But he was definitely a lot younger. I remember, at the time I wondered how surprising it was that Marjorie, of all people, should find a young toy boy, when richer and more glamorous older women could barely find a walker... let alone a lover." She shook her head in disbelief.

"Well, thank you, Mrs. Miller, that's certainly another lead we will be following up. I'd better make my way back to the police station. My colleagues here on the island have kindly given me an office in their headquarters from where I can operate. If you want to see me, just come into the police bureau and ask for me at the reception desk."

* * *

It took Gonzalez just a few minutes to walk the short distance from Worth Avenue to Golfview Road for his next appointment. It was time he had a word with Frederick Brownlow. He passed the Harvey residence, and before him loomed the imposing façade of yet another gracious historic house: 'Mon Repos', built by Maurice Fatio in 1928.

Gonzalez opened the ornate wrought iron gate and stepped through the meticulously kept front garden, to the heavily studded wooden entrance door. While he waited, he reminded himself with a sigh of a small task he had taken on to keep his wife happy.

Emilio Gonzalez was a thoroughly contented man: he loved Teresa and was perfectly happy living in the modest three-bedroom house in Plantation near Fort Lauderdale that they had purchased, preconstruction, four years ago. He could not see for the life of him the point of maintaining a huge residence, at exorbitant cost and with the added nightmare of keeping it safe. Mrs. Gonzalez, however, aspired to a more refined life style. She was intrigued by her husband's latest assignment and desired to know more about how the rich lived. Since Emilio had started working on this latest case among the very wealthy in Palm Beach, she had been cross-examining him every night about the people he met, their houses and their way of life.

It must be said that he had proved a sore disappointment to her so far. Carpets, curtains and other domestic details escaped him — unless a piece of furniture bore case-related fingerprints, he could never remember it. Hairstyles, jewelry and clothes remained a mere blur, unless these things were relevant to his work. But he had promised to do better today, and he was resolved to pay proper attention to everything he might have to describe later that night.

To his surprise the door was opened by Frederick Brownlow himself, a tall, severe looking, elderly man, very erect, wearing a well-cut blazer over a striped shirt. Having examined Gonzalez' identification he waved him in. "Follow me, Mr. Gonzalez. I am glad you were punctual."

They walked through a flagstone hallway and then into a large sitting room, furnished—so Gonzalez decided—in a French style, with several doors opening onto the garden. This was where his host led him, to a seating area under an enormous ficus tree. The garden brimmed with flowers, a tiled fountain (in the Spanish style?) splashed lustily and the view was inexorably drawn along the lawn to the distant fairways of the golf course beyond.

They took seats at a round wrought iron table with matching chairs and Gonzalez began his interrogation. His mournful expression was in odd contrast to the salubrious surroundings of 'Mon Repos' on this perfect Florida spring day.

"Mr. Brownlow, would you mind telling me a little about yourself and what you did on the morning of the murder?"

"Not at all. I live alone here. I am not married and have retired from most of my former business interests. I think it is fair to say that my life revolves around the Evergreen Club, which I have the honor of serving as president, as you are no doubt aware."

He stopped for a moment as if he wanted to give his visitor the chance to take in the enormity of this responsibility.

"On the morning in question, I got up at eight o'clock, as usual, and went to my study to make telephone calls. My housekeeper arrived at 8:30, but I normally don't see her until 10:30, when she brings me some tea and toast. I don't have any breakfast before that, but she would have heard me talking in my study and answering phone calls.

"At about twenty past nine our golf manager called me with the news of Osbert's discovery. I instantly went over to the club house, helped to identify the victim and spoke to the Palm Beach police officers who were there."

"Thank you, Mr. Brownlow. I don't know how to put this politely, but I understand that you and the deceased were not on particularly cordial terms."

"That is correct," admitted Brownlow without any further comment.

"I heard from someone, who shall remain nameless, that you and Mr. Robertson were seen, some years ago, sitting on a bench together, where an envelope apparently changed hands, from him to you or the other way around, and you were heard speaking in a foreign language. I'm sure there's a logical explanation... and wondered what you might have to say about it."

"Not much. Speaking in tongues? Exchanging envelopes? This sounds like a cheap detective novel. I don't know who told you this nonsense but I have no recollection of this incident and therefore cannot comment," was Brownlow's terse response.

"It is probably not important," admitted Gonzalez. "This is all for today. If I have more questions to ask you I will get in touch."

"Indeed, I'm sure you will. Feel free to call on me any time, but in the future, I think I would prefer to have my attorney present."

"As you wish, Mr. Brownlow." For once his hangdog expression was appropriate. "Thank you for seeing me." With these words, Gonzalez got up, but not without casting a last testing glance around the house and garden as he left the property.

CHAPTER 9

The Colony Hotel is not the biggest Hotel in Palm Beach (that would be the Breakers) nor the fanciest (that is arguably the Brazilian Court), but nevertheless it is a charming, popular hostelry in an enviably central location. Across the road—diagonally—is Worth Avenue, a few steps in the opposite direction is the beach. The pool area at the Colony is particularly attractive and usually busy, for lunch, for tea and especially in the early evening when guests and Palm Beach residents alike congregate for cocktails, often entertained by live music like a steel band.

At three o'clock on this lovely day in April the hotel was relatively quiet. Lunch was nearly over and the afternoon crowd had not yet arrived. Molly Miller drove up in her grey Toyota, left the car with the valet and entered the lobby. She had come to meet her friend Lucy. Her outfit today—as every day—was carefully chosen, and she presented a picture of discreet elegance. A cream-colored gabardine skirt (a little tight but all right as long as she remembered to pull in her stomach) was teamed with a cream silk shirt and a matching cardigan with very pretty little pearl buttons. Pearl earrings and a pearl bracelet completed the charming picture. Although she passed several large mirrors, Molly did not give herself the time to check her appearance, nor was she wasting even one admiring look, as she would normally do, at the splendid flower arrangement on the center table. The elevator took her up to the fifth floor and she found room 504 without difficulty. Her knock on the door was answered after a few seconds by a woman's voice, asking: "Who is it?"

"Lucy? It's Molly. I am sorry to disturb you like this. I wanted the receptionist to call you but he was busy and I was too impatient to wait. May I come in?"

"Of course, dear, how lovely to see you." Lucy de Silva, supported by her crutches, opened the door and stepped aside. The ladies exchanged air kisses, and Molly closed the door behind her. "I'm not too early, am I?"

"Well, I thought we were to meet in the lobby at 3:15 but I'm nearly ready. Make yourself comfortable, while I get my things together," answered Lucy.

"I'm so sorry to be early. I obviously got the time wrong," conceded Molly and carried on, changing the subject: "You do look nice, Lucy! This blue shirt from the 'Mouse' really suits you. I'm glad you bought it. You will be turning quite a few heads today."

Lucy shook her head, smiling. "I think those days have passed for me. I never expected to marry, being a cripple, but that never worried me. At least I had no horrible divorce to go through as so many of my friends did. And I did have a few, what you may call, meaningful relationships. But that was of course quite some time ago. Luckily we women don't need a man nowadays, or at least not a husband, to have a happy and fulfilled life."

Molly, thinking back with regret to her own blissful marriage, made only some noncommittal confirming noises and asked: "May I use your bathroom? I think I had too much coffee after lunch."

"Certainly, over there." Lucy pointed to an open door behind her.

When Molly returned after a moment, she commented: "What a pretty bathroom you have, so very elegant! And I must say, your bedroom is quite adorable. I'm glad you are so comfortable here."

"Yes, I'm very pleased with the hotel. At first I was disappointed not to have a view over the pool and to the sea. I had asked for it, but they must have misunderstood my request or muddled my booking. Anyway, I like looking over the golf course, and the road in front of the hotel is very quiet."

"Well, my dear, it's time to go. Have you decided which film you want to see?" asked Molly.

"Oh Molly, I'm afraid I have no idea. I haven't seen a movie for years. It will be such a treat just to be driven by you to West Palm and see City Place. I leave the choice of movies to you," answered her friend.

"Okay, there is one with Julia Roberts. She is quite a good actress but her huge mouth irritates me. And then there is one film with George Clooney—what do you think?" Lucy just shrugged her shoulders and Molly carried on: "I do like him, he reminds me of Jim—in his younger days of course. Yes, let's see George Clooney! By the way, I have a surprise for you. I had forgotten that I had accepted the invitation to a cocktail party tonight and rather then cancel it in the last minute, I asked whether I could bring you."

Lucy tried to interrupt her friend, but there was no stopping Molly.

"I know what you are trying to say. But I promise you, my friends will be delighted to meet you and you will like them. They are a rather unusual couple, you'll see, but their apartment alone is worth the visit. They live in an enormous penthouse at

Trump Plaza. That's in West Palm Beach and quite close to City Place, so we can go over to see them after the movie."

"Well my dear, it seems your plans are made. If you really think they won't mind my coming, I am game. Let's go!" The ladies took their bags, locked the door and made their way downstairs to the car.

* * * *

Emilio Gonzalez was walking slowly back along Golfview Road to the police headquarters. His thoughts went over his talk with Frederick Brownlow when someone behind him called his name: "Mr. Gonzalez? Agent Gonzalez?" He turned around and saw Sheila and Bill Wallace trying to catch up with him. They wore tennis whites, and he was carrying a large bag with rackets. They were clearly returning from a game at the Evergreen Club.

They looked like different people from the troubled couple he had met the other day at the Robertsons' house. He saw now what a lovely figure Sheila still had. The short skirt and sleeveless top suited her and displayed a gentle tan that she must have acquired very recently. Bill, Gonzalez had to admit, was a handsome man and from the way he looked today, sunburned, athletic and with a big smile, one could easily understand that once he had been the college heart throb. Gonzalez noticed with surprise that they were holding hands and looked clearly pleased to see him.

"Hello," he greeted them. "How are you? Did you have a good game of tennis?"

"Yes, thank you." Bill grinned. "It's been ages since we played together, but Sheila has lost none of her game. You know, she was really good when we met at college."

"Oh nonsense," she intercepted and pushed him playfully away from her. "I'm not good at all, but we had fun. Would you like to come in for a moment? It's so hot—I bet you could do with a cold drink," she added.

Gonzalez was not really interested in a drink but he nonetheless accepted. He considered it his duty to talk as much as possible to all of the people connected with the murder case, particularly anyone so closely involved. But he had another reason for wishing to visit the Robertsons' house again. He wanted to have a word with Gillian Fellows.

Sheila led the way into the garden room and Bill offered to get some drinks. Before he had even left the room, Sheila turned to Gonzalez and said with a smile: "I bet you're surprised to see us like this. Last time we met, we were all so chewed up about my father's death and other things. Of course, I'm still sad that Daddy died, and especially in that violent way. But strangely enough, I hope you don't mind my saying this, some good has come out of that tragic event.

"My brother is finally taking the step he should have taken years ago, which is to move back to the island and devote himself to art, his passion in life—not to mention certain people connected to the art world. And I… well, I don't quite know how to tell you this. Bill and I had, well, problems lately, the last few years really. I thought our marriage was over. He didn't seem interested in me anymore, and rather than forcing him to talk to me, I became shy and withdrew myself. What happened here made us scrutinize our lives, past and future, and I found out a lot of things that were totally new to me.

"Bill had been having business problems for some time. He is a very decent man, not perhaps as forceful and cunning as many of his colleagues. He felt undervalued at his job, got no promotions and was miserable because he thought he was letting me down—which is not at all true. Anyway, some time ago he had a great offer to go into partnership with some people he liked and trusted, but he needed some capital which he did not have. Silly man, he was too proud to ask me for help, but he felt desperate about letting such a wonderful opportunity slip by. So finally, when my father died, our emotional barriers came down, we talked about everything, how we felt about each other and about the way our life was going.

"When I heard about this business opportunity, I encouraged him to make some inquiries immediately. So the outcome of all this is, that they still want him to join, and on the strength of my inheritance, I can give him the financial backing that he needs... so, suddenly the future looks rosy. Bill has turned back into the man I fell in love with, and it seems that he never stopped loving me. Now, at least, he is showing it again and we simply could not be happier. Willie sees what is going on and you can observe how he is coming out of his protective shell. He and Bill had a long 'man to man' chat last night, and I am sure in time they will build a good, strong father and son-relationship. Well, that was a long talk... and here comes Bill, bringing ice cold drinks."

She took the offered glass. "I drink to the future. May the murderer be caught! Cheers!"

"I second that." Bill Wallace raised his glass and Gonzalez followed his example.

"I wish I could tell you that the case is almost solved but it isn't. However, we've got some promising leads, and I have no doubt that whoever did this, will not get away with it. Meanwhile, I drink to your very good health and fortune." Something resembling a smile lit up his doleful features. "By the way," Gonzalez carried on, "we received some interesting information about your housekeeper. It seems that Mrs. Pitt has a much younger lover in her life. Do you know anything about that?"

Sheila gave him a big smile. "I have news for you, Chief Detective. Marjorie is not nearly as wicked as you make us believe or, shall I say, as lucky as that. The so-called lover is her son, a rather wayward young man who until recently lived with his father in, I don't quite remember, I think Seattle. Marjorie came to talk to us last night. She explained the situation and asked us whether we would allow her to have her son live with her at least for a while. We met him earlier this morning and he doesn't seem a bad lot. What did you think, Bill?"

Bill Wallace agreed. "No, I rather liked him. We are quite happy to have him live with Marjorie. There is enough room, and in return, he wants to do odd jobs around the house which is a blessing. You know, these old houses are beautiful but crumbling, and need constant attention. Young Pitts seems to have a practical knack and has promised to start right away painting a few flaking window frames and such. If it also keeps Marjorie happy, all the better."

"Oh, that's very interesting," Gonzalez said. "I'm glad you told me. But there's something else, Mrs. Wallace, that needs clearing up. Is your uncle at home? I would like to see him if possible."

"Oh yes, I think he and Morreen are at the pool. Shall I call them or would you like to go over there?" Sheila, noticing his dark, crumpled suit, couldn't help teasing him. "Would you like to take a dip? I am sure we could find you some bathing trunks."

Gonzalez looked at her with horror and his sorrow lines appeared deeper than ever. "No, no, thank you. I am on duty and swimming is not one of my leisure activities. But with your permission I'll make my way over to the pool. I know where it is. And thank you for the drink! No doubt, I'll be in touch again soon."

Gonzalez wound his way cautiously through the exotic blooms, past citrus trees in huge terra cotta pots and stone urns brimming with extravagant color towards the pool area. Even from quite a distance away he could hear laughter and splashing. When he stepped through the arched opening of the hedge surrounding the pool, he found himself an involuntary witness to a charming scene.

Gil Fellows, in shorts and T-shirt, was basking on a comfortable chaise lounge, half shaded by a green and white striped umbrella and further protected by a straw hat and sun glasses. He had a book in his hand, and several other volumes plus papers were stacked on the floor. His friend Morreen was in the pool, hanging onto the edge with one hand and playfully splashing water towards her companion with the other. All this was accompanied by loud protests from Gil and laughter from Morreen, who continued with the game.

Gonzalez stopped and could not help smiling. Morreen saw him first and waved to him, inviting him to come closer. As she pulled herself out of the water, he noticed her perfect body - smooth long limbs, flat stomach, small, firm breasts – which were freely displayed in a microscopic white bikini.

His mind conjured up the short, sturdy figure of his life's companion. Teresa was a traditionally built woman who favored ample black swim suits with little skirts. Sylphlike she was not but, he reminded himself, she was a woman with sterling qualities, strength of character, loyalty…

With a start he pulled himself out of his reverie and back to the present.

He saw that Gil Fellows raised a languid hand to offer another pool chaise to their visitor. Gonzalez looked like a large, black bird as he crouched gingerly on it, briefcase on the floor next to his leg, pen and paper in his hand.

"I wanted to have a word with you, Mr. Fellows, if that's convenient now." He looked nervously over to Morreen who shook out her long tresses in an attempt to dry herself. She caught his eye and quickly announced that she would go back to the house and change.

"Mr. Fellows, is it true that you had an argument with your brother-in-law on the night of your arrival, just hours before he was murdered?"

"Yes, I did," Gil readily admitted. "May I ask how you know about it?"

"It's no secret. Mrs. Pitts, who has, of course, a set of keys for the house, came back late at night because she had forgotten her cell phone in the pantry. She heard loud voices from the library. Naturally she was curious and listened for a moment until she had identified the speakers as her boss, Mr. Robertson, and you. She felt it was her duty to tell me about it," was Gonzalez' answer.

"That's quite all right. So, you want to know what we talked about?" Gil looked speculatively at the special agent.

Encouraged by a nod he continued: "I never understood why my lovely sister married this uptight, boring man, but there we are. Strangely enough they were quite happy, and that was enough for me. And I have to admit, their kids are great. When Elizabeth died, it was a terrible shock for all of us. After the funeral I asked Frank, whether I could have some of the antique snuff bottles that my father had left to Elizabeth. After all they came from my family and I felt I had a right to them. I would have sold one or two of them, which would have been useful, and kept the rest. Needless to say, Frank was most indignant and refused point blank. What really annoyed me was the fact that he was not even particularly interested in the damned things—he just wanted to hang onto them because of their value. We all like money, but he was just a greedy old bastard—excuse my French. Well, to make a long story short, I tried my luck again. I need something to tide myself over until my novel is published, and I thought old age had perhaps mellowed my charming brother-in-law. But no! He was adamant that I had no right, moral or otherwise, to his precious bottles. We had a bit of a shouting match, and I told him what I thought of him and vice versa. That was all. I left the study, slammed the door and went to bed."

With a smile he added: "And I did not spend the night making plans how best to bump him off."

"And what did you do the following morning before breakfast? You left the house just after eight and came back shortly before nine. I know, you went jogging but did anybody see you? Where did you run?"

Gil looked uncertain. "I ran along the beach. There were lots of people, but I can't think of anyone specific."

"Don't worry about it." Gonzalez got up. "Maybe we can find someone who remembers you, the beach guard perhaps or one of the doormen along South Ocean Boulevard. Thank you for your time. Good bye."

Gil gave a little wave and sank back, gratefully, into his chaise.

* * *

Punctually at 6:15 p.m., Mrs. Miller and her friend left the cinema at the Muvico complex at City Place, in West Palm Beach. The film had not been quite to the ladies' liking. They would have preferred fewer car chases, much less violence and shooting, and more romance and tap dancing. With a sigh Molly remembered the movies she and Mr. Miller had treasured above all: *Casablanca*, *Gone With the Wind* and her all-time favorite: *Singing in the Rain*.

"I don't know about you, Lucy, but I thought that was disappointing. Too much sex and violence, and not enough romance. It's the same with books. So often I try a new novel and then I can't even finish it. Usually, that means I go back to reread something from my favorite author, Georgette Heyer. Are you familiar with her?" The ladies walked slowly towards the parking garage.

"I don't think so. I personally love the classics above all. Give me Shakespeare any time!" was Lucy's answer.

"Lucky you!" Once again Molly was full of admiration for her clever friend. "I once saw a production of 'Romeo and Juliet' with Jim, which was perfectly lovely, although I confess I cried a lot because it was so sad. But in general I find Shakespeare's language rather difficult. Do you have a favorite?" she asked.

"Yes, 'Hamlet'," Lucy answered promptly.

"This is not a play I am particularly familiar with," Molly confessed, "and the little I remember is not altogether to my liking. Isn't there a ghost in it? And some chaps digging graves?" She shuddered. "We have enough of that right here. Poor Francis was buried yesterday. I do wish they had caught the murderer!" Lucy nodded in agreement.

The ladies got into the Toyota and drove the short distance to their party at Trump Tower.

* * *

Ambassador Don Balduccio and Senora Maria-Victoria Garcia received their friends in the first of two interconnecting reception rooms of grand proportions. They had managed to buy the two best penthouses in the building and connect them, thereby creating a palatial space with a sensational view, a setting adequate even for a former sugar princess from Cuba. They had also enclosed the original wraparound balconies, which had enlarged the rooms and increased the impact of the view by placing the enormous plate glass windows at the very edge of the tower's perimeter.

Stepping out of the private elevator, guests were welcomed into the octagonal marble hallway by two butlers who took the guests' coats away and offered them drinks. Continuing towards the light and laughter, they appeared before the host and hostess, who greeted every one of their friends warmly. Senora Garcia kissed those she knew, and extended her richly adorned hand graciously towards newcomers. Her husband delighted the ladies with charmingly performed kisses that hovered just above their hands.

Molly ushered her friend in. Lucy was painfully aware of the noise her crutches made on the marble floor, but everybody was polite enough not to stare as she was introduced to their hosts. They exchanged pleasantries and then stepped aside when the next group of guests advanced.

Like all first time visitors, Lucy was magically drawn to the windows which afforded a sweeping 180-degree view, up and down the Intracoastal Waterway, over the island of Palm Beach and towards the distant ocean. The sun was beginning to set and poured liquid red-gold over the paradisiacal land- and sea-scapes below.

Only once she had sufficiently admired the view, did Lucy de Silva begin to take in the details of her surroundings. During the few days she had spent in Palm Beach, she had seen houses and vistas of great beauty, but the grand display here, inside and out, took her breath away.

Molly watched her friend with a smile. "Aren't you glad we came?" As Lucy nodded, she carried on: "These two, despite their riches—if I may say so—are very, very dear people, and everybody treasures their invitations, because they are so generous but also very much loved. Isn't Marivi—that's what everybody calls her—adorable? As you can see she is not a young woman, about my age I would say, but just look at her: how simply stunning she is!"

Lucy had to agree: Marivi carried her voluptuous figure with a majestic grace. Two great assets contributed to her startling appearance: her flawless complexion, which was a gift of nature, and her spectacular jewelry, which was, on the other hand, man-made. It had come originally from her own family and had been amply augmented over the years by her doting husband.

Today an emerald green velvet dress displayed a generous amount of cleavage, showing an ample alabaster bosom, bedecked with an opulent necklace of diamonds and emeralds the size of big cherries. This formed a spectacular contrast to her chestnut red hair, piled high on her head.

Her husband, in contrast, was a small, spare man, who gave an overall impression of grey—hair, face, clothes—until you noticed his eyes, twinkling with good humor.

He was in every way the perfect foil for his adored wife. He was plain and calm, so she could be all the more flamboyant and sparkling.

Don Balduccio hailed from a rich Venezuelan family. As he did not care for business and was well provided for by his family, he had served his country as ambassador to such challenging superpowers as Togo, Albania and Belize. Life had been mildly dull until the day he encountered his fate in the shapely form of Maria-Victoria. The recently widowed Marivi had caught his eye one night at Club Colette and for him, that was it. He pursued her ardently and relentlessly until finally, one happy day, she consented to become his wife. Since then it had been his mission to spoil and indulge and worship her—the love of his life.

Marivi had been a raven-haired Latin beauty who, at the death of her first husband, "went red with grief." Although Florida had been her home for forty years, Spanish was still her first language, and home would always be Havana. Her two best friends, Lourdes and Carmelita, had been at school with her, and as they were all now living in Palm Beach, they continued to see each other at least once a week for lunch.

Their first husbands, the fathers of their children, had all died. Lourdes and Carmelita were now married to "gringos", good providers, and perhaps better and more faithful partners, if somewhat less exciting than their first loves.

Marivi, despite her tangible happiness with the lucky Balduccio, occasionally still lamented her first husband, Ernesto, who had suffered a hero's death: playing polo in Wellington, he fell off his pony and died, instantly and decorously.

Cubans, even in lifelong exile, never lose their love for music and entertaining. Feeling euphoric or despairing—either was a good enough reason to give a party. The food, cooked at home by their Cuban staff, was delicious and ample, the margaritas flowed and Marivi, Lourdes and Carmelita tangoed with the best of them.

Music was provided by a little band in another reception room. With a violin, trumpet, guitar and a piano, they played Latin tunes, singing and providing great entertainment. The musicians wore embroidered, short black jackets with silver buttons and long red bow ties.

Two couples, who had already started dancing, were clearly keen and skilled: they swept across the floor with staccato footwork, holding their upper bodies erect, showing full concentration on their faces.

Molly and Lucy listened and watched attentively. Molly, who knew no Spanish, could only distinguish the odd "ole" and heard something like *La Bamba*. She smiled at her friend. "Marivi loves music and dancing. She usually has this little orchestra, which she calls... wait... something like 'Marianchi', I believe."

"Mariachi," corrected Lucy without thinking. "Yes, I have heard this type of music before. It really gets into your blood, doesn't it?"

Molly did her best to introduce Lucy to some of her friends. And indeed Lucy, who had first been reluctant to come, was now thoroughly enjoying herself.

She was fascinated by this whole new, strange, colorful world. There was a predominance of Latin guests, with Spanish being used more commonly than English.

Molly pointed out a few more prominent guests and took Lucy around to meet them, until she noticed that her friend looked tired. "How are you feeling, my dear?" she asked solicitously. "Have we overdone it? Maybe we should call it a day."

Lucy agreed that she was ready to leave. The ladies had enjoyed the cocktail food offered so much, they had no need for dinner.

They said good bye to their hosts and made their way downstairs and back to the island.

CHAPTER 10

TUESDAY

"Who isse speaking? Isse nobody at home." After the telephone had rung about ten times, Manolita had finally decided to answer it, but with an evident lack of eagerness. Gonzalez repeated his name and tried in vain to catch Manolita's ear in Spanish. He wanted to know when Mrs. Miller was expected back home.

"No sé. Nobody tell me nothing. Adios." Without waiting for Gonzalez to say anything further, and without even realizing that he was addressing her in her own language, she hung up.

At that very moment the front door opened, and Mrs. Miller entered her apartment. She had returned from a bimonthly engagement of singular importance, second only to dates with Henry Standing: a visit to Jean-Christophe. He was the Number One hair artist on the island. Luckily she had been visiting him for nearly all of the twenty-five years that his salon had been open. For "new" ladies trying to get an appointment, it was now as difficult as joining an elite club. Molly swore by Jean-Christophe. He was the only one who knew how to control her hair and preserve the rich brown sheen of her youth. But apart from his skill with scissors and dye, he was an inexhaustible source of news, and thus indispensable to Molly. He was everybody's confidant, and knew facts and figures, where others had heard only vague rumors. Anything newsworthy came his way and as he regarded it as wonderfully important, he passed it on without malice. Thus, immaculately coiffed and fully armed with up to date information, Molly Miller was ready to tackle the day and the tasks ahead.

"Hello Manolita," she called, discreetly sniffing the smoke-filled air. "Did I hear you speaking on the telephone? Was that for me?"

"Si Senora... the policia. Chief Gonzalez. He want to speak to you."

"Oh I see, thank you, Manolita. I'll call him back."

"Are you all right?" she asked nervously as Manolita was racked by an attack of smoker's cough.

"Isse ok," Manolita gasped. "Isse the air conditioning, make me sick." Thus grumbling, she retreated into her kitchen.

"Special Agent Gonzalez, please." Mrs. Miller said to the operator at the Palm Beach Police Department. "This is Mrs. Miller speaking."

After a moment the agent's voice was heard. "Thank you for calling me back, Mrs. Miller. I wanted to talk to you again, because I must confess that we have reached a bit of a dead end with our investigation into Mr. Francis Robertson's death. I just wonder whether you have found out anything that could help us."

Mrs. Miller sat down comfortably, with an expression of happy anticipation on her face. "Well, Special Agent Gonzalez, why don't you tell me first how far you have gotten."

"The trouble is, we have so little to go on. For me, frankly, the butler is the most likely suspect. With his gambling habit, he probably needs cash more than anybody else. He stands to gain quite a lot from the legacy, of which he was well aware. He also would have known where his boss kept his cash, and who is to say whether or not he helped himself to some of that? He knows Robertson's habits. He could easily have slipped out of the house for five minutes. That's all the time he needed to cross the road, kill him, and return."

"Well, I don't know." It was now Mrs. Miller's turn. "I have come across one or two little intriguing facts, but nothing concrete. I've been giving it a lot of thought. May I make a suggestion? How would you feel if we arranged a meeting with everybody who is even vaguely connected to the case, and who was near the crime scene?

"We could reconstruct the murder, go over everybody's movements at the time, and I would not be surprised if someone let slip a remark that will substantially help us solve the case.

"I propose that you notify everybody, and ask them to convene tomorrow evening at the Golf Pavilion of the Evergreen Club. Another day should give you sufficient time to complete your research of everybody's background. Tomorrow is Wednesday, and on that day the luncheon room is closed after six o'clock. I am sure they would keep it open for you on that occasion.

"At this meeting, all the suspects can confront each other, any lies will be detected, hopefully, and I feel very strongly that we will be able to discover the murderer right there and then. What do you think?"

There was such a long silence that Mrs. Miller wondered whether Gonzalez was still on the line. Finally she heard his answer.

"Well, it certainly couldn't hurt. All right, I'll ask everybody to meet us tomorrow evening at seven o'clock in the Golf

Pavilion. Thank you, Mrs. Miller, I'll see you then and there."

"Oh Agent Gonzalez, excuse me, are you planning to invite Birdie Baker as well? I know she really has nothing to do with the case as such, but you never know, it might be helpful," added Molly.

"Indeed, Mrs. Miller, I see no problem about having her with us. And the same goes for your friend, Mrs. de Silva. She is clearly an innocent outsider, but as she was so close by, meeting with you at the time of the attack, you might want to bring her too."

"Thank you. I'll invite her then. I shall see you tomorrow."

CHAPTER 11

WEDNESDAY

At a quarter of seven the next evening, Special Agent in Charge Emilio Gonzalez waited at the Golf Pavilion of the Evergreen Club. A few of his fellow officers were stationed discreetly at different places nearby, on the patio, at the entrance to the pro shop and in the parking lot. Several tables had been moved together, with chairs grouped around to provide seats for close to twenty people. On a side table were some bottles of water and glasses for self service. No waiters or waitresses were in attendance.

The first to turn up were Sheila and Bill Wallace, with their son Willie. Bill had his arm draped around his wife's shoulder. They were clearly relishing their newfound happiness and status. Even Willie's habitual adolescent scowl had been replaced with an expression almost resembling amiability. They greeted Gonzalez, and taking some water to the table, sat down at one end.

The Wallaces were followed in by Mr. and Mrs. Harris. Martin tried to conceal some evident discomfort with his usual rather noisy bonhomie. His wife Peggy nodded towards Gonzalez and took a seat next to Sheila, whom she greeted with a kiss.

As the time approached seven, the door opened and closed several more times in quick succession. Sam Robertson appeared with Marylou and her mother Birdie, who had Osbert Harvey in tow. Marylou's outfit was unobtrusive as always, something dark and comfortable. Birdie, however, had clearly taken trouble to dress for the occasion: black narrow trousers, a black and white striped shirt with a black cardigan. Even her lipstick was more muted than usual.

Osbert Harvey had also taken the sobriety of the occasion into consideration for his choice of attire: grey flannel trousers, with a crease that could cut bread, were teamed with a dove grey silk shirt and a blazer. The inevitable kerchief fluttered from his breast pocket. Sam's look was a more profound trans-formation—in the absence of his father's rigid dress code, he appeared truly relaxed in jeans and a sweater, long hair flopping over his forehead.

The unmistakable click-clack of Lucy de Silva's crutches announced her approach. Molly Miller opened the door for her friend and helped her to find a seat at the table. Molly greeted everybody and looked expectantly around the table. "Isn't Henry coming?" she wanted to know.

"I am here, Molly dear," came a voice from the entrance. Henry Standing rushed through the room and clasped his friend affectionately in his arms. He was looking particularly debonair and clearly struck a note with Molly. A blue linen suit was teamed with a pink shirt and a paisley-patterned bow tie.

"Henry, you really have such wonderful taste. No man in Palm Beach dresses like you," she sighed.

"I should hope not," he answered, with a twinkle in his eye, "because nobody has a tie like this. Don't you remember? You gave it to me for my birthday."

146

"So I did," confirmed Molly with a slight blush. "I have never seen you wear it before. But it certainly suits you."

"May I return the compliment?" asked the gallant Henry. "Molly, my dear, you have never looked more fetching. Perhaps it's time we took another little trip in my motorcar."

"That would be lovely," Molly readily agreed.

She was her usual delightful picture of soignée girlishness. She wore a yellow piqué suit with a narrow skirt and a simple short jacket, with a becoming Peter Pan collar. The finishing touch was a short necklace of big pearls.

Gonzalez looked around him. There were still some empty seats left. He decided to wait another instant. Just then the door opened and Frederick Brownlow appeared, looking displeased and bored. Gonzalez went out of his way to be friendly and welcoming, but the club president was in no mood for pleasantries. With a short nod to everybody, he took a seat and tapped his fingers impatiently on the table.

The general attention was drawn to the door when it swung open with aplomb. Gil Fellows strode in with Morreen bustling behind him. Gil gave a general, cheery hello and waved to Sheila and Sam. He wore jeans like his nephew, a striped shirt, blazer and Gucci loafers without socks, as was the unwritten rule for gentlemen in Palm Beach. This Agatha Christie-inspired meeting had appealed so much to Morreen and her sense of the dramatic that she had decided to make her appearance stage-worthy. She was a picture of bohemian chic, from top to toe: her hair tousled, tweaked and adorned with flowers, her feet in towering platform sandals with ribbons wound around her shapely calves. Instead of a skirt she had a sarong knotted around her waist which opened seductively with every tottering step she took. A see-through shirt that revealed most of her delectable breasts completed the ensemble. The men all swallowed hard and Martin Harris found it difficult to take his eyes off her. Brownlow simply raised an eyebrow and bowed his head into his hand in dismay.

The last to arrive were Maurice Dutroix and Marjorie Pitts, who looked serious and seemed tense. They greeted Gonzalez and sat down quietly.

Rather than take the last empty chair at the table, Special Agent in Charge Gonzalez remained standing as he addressed the assembled group.

"Thank you all for coming tonight. You know why we are here. A man who has lived in your midst for many years, a friend, a neighbor, has been brutally murdered. We want to try and find out who killed Mr. Francis Robertson. As some of you know, the primary murder investigation is being conducted by officers of the local police force, but many of you must be speculating about why I was drafted into the case.

"As I explained to some of you, there are certain 'special circumstances' under which the FBI is brought in to assist in a local investigation..." This comment set off murmuring and whispering among the assembled group. "We are also sensitive to the fact that when the Bureau is brought in, it tends to arouse more suspicion about the victim's background than it does about any of the possible suspects." Gonzalez paused briefly and let one more wave of murmurs circle the table.

"As you may know, the Bureau cooperates with local law enforcement and investigates crimes that may involve such things as counter intelligence, public corruption, organized crime, art theft, environmental crimes, money laundering, various types of white-collar crime... including securities, bankruptcy and insurance fraud. If a victim or a suspect has had any prior involvement with a crime that may have been investigated by the Bureau, it might warrant our involvement..."

"In this particular case, it seems that Frank Robertson had once been investigated by the FBI. As you know, he spent a lot of his time and money collecting Chinese porcelain. To this effect he traveled occasionally to Hong Kong, but also to mainland China, the source of all really valuable Imperial ware. There was a suspicion that the Chinese had tried to buy his services... He just seemed too lucky in the art work he managed to buy, privately, from dealers and at auctions. But ultimately no proof of foul play was found. This is how I came to be involved in the case. Among many other leads, we looked into this Far East connection again, but had to drop it for lack of evidence.

"A lot of speculation went on about the motive for the murder. As you all know, Mr. Robertson was a wealthy man. But the assault did not take place to rob him. As far as we know, nothing was taken from his person by the killer. Quite a few people, however, knew that they stood to benefit from his death. He is leaving a lot of money to his heirs, his family and to a lesser degree, to Mrs. Pitts and Mr. Dutroix.

"This kept bringing us back to suspecting that the killer was probably from his own circle of family, friends, or neighbors. And this is where you come in. I need your help, and I am convinced you all will give it to me, except that is, for one person... the murderer. Because it is more than likely that he is here tonight, amongst us."

Everybody stirred uncomfortably. "All of you knew his habits, his daily golf game every morning. Of course it is possible that an outsider acquainted himself with Mr. Robertson's routine. In fact, I found out that a stranger did show some suspicious interest in the life and habits of the victim. Someone was making pointed inquiries regarding Frank Robertson."

He paused for a moment and then continued: "Mr. Dutroix, will you repeat for all of us here what you told me earlier?"

The butler cleared his throat and began to speak hesitatingly, evidently nervous. "When the agent interrogated me, I told him that some months ago I met a man at the dog races who asked me all sorts of questions about the late Mr. Robertson. First I paid no attention to him and avoided giving specific answers. But after a while... we had a few drinks and he seemed a decent enough fellow..."

Dutroix seemed uncertain how to continue. "This man, as I said, I had not met him before, he was not from this area, but he claimed to have met Mr. Robertson, and he asked me all these things because he wanted to ascertain that it was indeed the same man. There didn't seem to be any harm in that. Of course I would never have talked about security arrangements at the house or whether there were valuables or anything like that."

"Would you recognize this man if we showed you some photographs?" asked the special agent.

Dutroix shook his head. "I doubt it. It was quite dark in the room. He was middle-aged, I don't know, elderly perhaps, not too tall and he wore a hat. Quite well-dressed, I seem to remember, but there was nothing memorable or unusual about the man, and I never saw him again."

"Thank you, Mr. Dutroix, that will do for the moment. At this stage we don't know whether this mysterious stranger is involved in the murder or not. But let's go back to the morning of the murder. According to everything we know and especially to the testimony of Mr. Standing, Frank Robertson was last seen alive at 8:35 a.m. He would normally have left the golf course at 8:55. For these twenty minutes nearly everybody has an alibi. This is the most puzzling aspect of the case."

Gonzalez paused and woefully studied the water glass in his hand.

Molly Miller looked up and said: "Agent Gonzalez, it seems that the time factor depends entirely on Henry's observation. Of course, dear Henry is totally above suspicion. But what if he made a mistake?" She made a dramatic pause.

"Dearest Molly," Henry Standing objected, "I can assure you that my watch is one hundred percent accurate."

"I don't doubt that," she replied. "What I mean is, maybe the person who waved to Henry wasn't Frank at all? What do we know? Henry expected to see Frank, remember? As long as someone looked like Frank, was dressed like Frank and waved to him as Frank always did, it would not have occurred to him to doubt that this was indeed Frank Robertson." Turning to Henry, she asked, "Henry, was there any reason why the person that you saw, had to have been Frank?"

"Well, if you put it like that..." Henry Standing was clearly puzzled. "It just never crossed my mind..." He shook his head. "Frank always wore beige chinos, a polo shirt and his blue cap. What DID surprise me that day, now that I think back on it, was how well Frank... well, whoever it was... the man I took for Frank... played! You know, the 13th hole is a par 4 and normally Frank used an iron and got no further than, let's say, 120 yards. That morning, however, he hit the ball brilliantly, and came quite close to the green. I thought at the time, the old boy must have taken a lesson or two." With an apologetic look to Sheila and Sam he added: "I am sorry, my dears."

"OK, let's explore that line of reasoning..." said Gonzalez, with a little nod to Molly. "If we accept this new possibility, that the man hitting off the 13th tee at 8:35 was not Francis Robertson, we might have to consider two things. First, that this person was the murderer, and secondly that Mr. Robertson was already dead by then."

Deadly silence fell over the assembled group. Then everybody started talking at once. Obvious disbelief, surprise, and shock showed on their faces. Birdie looked wide-eyed with horror at Osbert, who dabbed his forehead with his silk handkerchief. Bill Wallace took his wife's hand. Sam looked at Marylou. Only Frederick Brownlow seemed not only disinterested, but positively bored.

Molly Miller alone had a slight smile on her face. None of what she just heard was a surprise to her. She glanced over at Lucy, but her friend continued to rummage in her handbag, until she extracted some peppermints.

Once again Gonzalez' soulful expression was appropriate. He raised his hand and waited for the chatter to subside.

"The body was discovered between the 18th tee and the 13th green. So far we were assuming that Robertson was killed after playing the 13th hole and before he had time to play the 18th, at roughly 8:40. But now we have to revise this estimate. It seems he was murdered earlier, after having played the 10th hole, which would have been at about 8:15. Now we have to go back and recheck everybody's alibi for this new, earlier time."

Special Agent Gonzalez turned around to face Martin Harris. "If you don't mind, Mr. Harris, let's start with you. You told us that you did not leave your house until you departed with your wife at ten of nine to drive the short distance to Golfview Road. This was confirmed by your wife. But this is not exactly correct, is it?" Gonzalez waited for a moment while Martin Harris, clearly uncomfortable, shifted in his seat. Peggy looked attentively at him but remained silent.

"Your wife wouldn't necessarily have known if you had gone out earlier, quietly, would she? And this is what you did, isn't that right? You were seen on Golfview Road shortly after eight. This didn't make you a suspect at first, because the murder was supposed to have been committed later. However, now that we have revised the time of the crime, you were right there at the time of the murder... and you lied about it."

"Since you know I was there, I might as well come clean about it." Martin Harris pushed his chair back, crossed his arms defiantly and spoke without hesitation.

"I went to Golfview Road that morning to catch Frank on his way to the golf course. I thought that was the only chance I ever had to see him alone. I knew that during breakfast I wouldn't be able to talk to him in private.

"And yes, I wanted to try and persuade him to sell the house and let me do a conversion job, but there was nothing fraudulent or underhanded about it. I knew he paid through the nose to keep that huge house running. He had complained more than once about it to me. I was going to give him a very generous price for it. The banks would advance me the money because I would have been able to make a lot of money dividing the property into several smaller dwellings. I have done it before, and it was a great success... for everybody. I need money, I admit it. I tried to do some business. It failed.

"When I arrived at Frank's house on the morning of the murder, he had already left. I just saw him entering the club and I knew I was too late. I turned around to go home and planned to try meeting him alone another time.

"By the way, my wife didn't know that I had left the house. I did not tell her about my plans, because I didn't want to worry her with money troubles. She didn't lie to you." Peggy looked at him with a tender expression and put her hand consolingly on his shoulder.

Gonzalez nodded. "Thank you, Mr. Harris. Let's turn to you now, Mr. Fellows. By your own admission you had a heated argument with your brother-in-law on the night of your arrival at his house. The next morning you went jogging, from just after eight, until shortly before nine. You cannot remember having met anybody you know during that time, and we couldn't find anyone who saw you. Moreover, I understand that when you returned, you barely looked flushed, not at all like a man who has been running for fifty minutes. Please tell us what you were doing during that time period."

Once again ominous silence settled on the room. Everybody looked at Gillian. He raised his head and said defiantly: "I cannot tell you. You just have to believe me that I had nothing to do with Frank's death."

Molly cut in gently. "Maybe someone else can shed some light on Gillian's movements that morning."

After a brief moment, Birdie's nervous voice was heard. "Gillian was with me—the whole time—from ten past eight, until a quarter of nine."

Everybody turned to stare at Birdie, who suddenly looked flushed and uncomfortable. "We... we are old friends, and had something to talk about. Anyway, this is all that needs to be said. Gillian wasn't anywhere near the golf course. I swear it."

Gillian got up from his chair and fetched himself some water. Damn, he thought to himself, I couldn't have chosen a worse time to see Birdie, and now I have embarrassed her. Would this now be the end?

While the others talked to each other in muted tones, he looked over to Birdie and tried to catch her eye. He was fonder of her than ever. How could he have ever left her? In all the years that he had visited Palm Beach, Birdie had been a good friend. When he came to Elizabeth's funeral, he was desperate with grief and she had been a tower of strength. During those days, their friendship had become a love affair. And yet, he had returned to New York, leaving her, not even writing to her for many months. His fear of commitment had overruled all other feelings. There had been other women, and then Morreen... But

154

lately he had been thinking of Birdie more and more, of the fun they had had together, and of her tenderness during that time of his loss. When he finally decided to come back to Palm Beach, he knew he wanted to see her again.

It was brave of her to admit his visit, to give him an alibi. She knew that this would inevitably lead to gossip. Tongues had started wagging when they spent so much time together after Elizabeth's death. She would hardly enjoy once again being linked with him. Would she want to see him ever again after this? Brooding over his predicament, Gil went back to his chair, not daring to look at Morreen.

Gonzalez was continuing to unravel the events of the fatal morning. "Now we have explanations for Mr. Harris' and Mr. Fellow's movements. The other family members were either in their rooms, like Mrs. Wallace and her brother, or in the garden. Mr. Wallace spent the early morning reading at the pool. Miss Morreen told me she never left the garden. This was confirmed by the butler and the housekeeper who saw her bright red kaftan near the fountain where she burned incense and meditated.

"Oh yes, but there is still young Willie." All eyes turned in his direction and he shifted nervously in his chair. Gonzalez went on, "Well, I have never come across a youngster of his age who is up voluntarily before midday. Even the breakfast at nine o'clock made huge demands on him, and so we can safely believe him, when he says that he was fast asleep until his mother dragged him out of bed at 8:55." Everybody smiled.

"But our investigations have brought some more interesting facts to light. Mrs. Miller informed me of a curious scene she witnessed several years ago, which I would like to bring to your attention. Some of you may be aware of the fact that the late Mr. Robertson was not on friendly terms with Mr. Brownlow." He looked at the club president, who showed no emotions whatsoever and shrugged his shoulders.

"Mrs. Miller informs me that she recalled seeing the two gentlemen sitting together on a bench, talking. She noticed that an envelope changed hands, and when she passed close by, she caught some words being spoken in a foreign language." He turned to Molly. "Is that correct?"

"Yes it is," confirmed Mrs. Miller.

"Would you like to comment on this, Mr. Brownlow?" Gonzalez asked.

"No thank you. I find this whole meeting here tonight unnecessary and intrusive. All I wish to say is, that I have nothing whatsoever to do with the murder and you can believe it or not, just as you wish," was Brownlow's answer.

"I am sorry that you feel so negative, Mr. Brownlow. I hope we don't need to keep you all here for too long. Please exercise a little more patience.

"Our investigations into your past brought to light that you, Mr. Brownlow, were born in Berlin. After the war you came to the States. You changed your name from Braunschweig to Brownlow. You went to school here, never mentioned your birthplace, and did everything you could to give the impression that you were a born and bred American. Please, don't misunderstand me. There is nothing reprehensible in that.

"You settled in Palm Beach after you took early retirement from a successful career as a stock broker. Golf is your passion, and you went out of your way to involve yourself with the Evergreen Club. You worked hard, and eventually your dream came true: they asked you to become president of this prestigious club.

"Your prized position was put into jeopardy after just a few years. Francis Robertson turned up in Palm Beach, of all the people in the world, and he recognized you. Like you, he came from Berlin, from the same neighborhood. He had also immigrated to the United States a long time ago and become

American. But there was one problem: He knew that you are a Jew."

There was a short intake of breath from Sheila, and voices rose. Surprise, disbelief... all heads turned to Frederick Brownlow. His face had taken on a death-white pallor. With a weary movement, he shook his head and started to speak.

"That's right. My parents were Jewish, and I was brought up in the Jewish faith until I came to America. I was given new papers and they stated 'Episcopalian' as my religion. I am not a churchgoer, as you all know. I am not an atheist, I am an agnostic. The question of my religion never came up in New York. When I moved to Palm Beach, a long time ago, social mores were not what they are today. It was imperative then, that nobody should know about my past, my early childhood. All went well, until Franz turned up. Franz Roberts, my neighborhood pal! Of all the places in the world, he settled in Palm Beach, on the very street where I was living. I tried to pretend that he had made a mistake, but he knew. He knew who I was, and he wanted to create mischief. It amused him that someone with my background was president of the ultraconservative, gentile Evergreen Club. And once he realized how important my position was to me, he could not resist teasing me, tantalizing me.

"He knew he had the power to destroy me socially, and he reveled in that power. He began to blackmail me. First he just made demands to do with the club. He always had to have the best table, insisted on being on every committee he chose, and eventually he became mercantile. He asked me for the odd $1,000 here and there. It was not that he needed the money, he just loved being in a position to threaten and scare me.

"When Molly saw us, it must have been one of those occasions when I handed over some cash to him—not that I recall that particular time."

Frederick Brownlow looked at Sheila and Sam. "I am sorry if you are hearing about a side of your father that you might not like to know. What I am telling you is the absolute truth. But that does not make me a murderer. Yes, I disliked Franz, or Francis as he liked to be known, I even hated him at times, but it never occurred to me to take his life.

"His taunting had been going on for years, and I was pretty certain he would not follow through with his threats. It would not have done him any favors to come out with the truth after so many years. I had almost gotten used to the situation and anyway, his demands had become less frequent as the years went on. Even he got bored with the game, I guess. I swear to you that I am not his murderer." With these words he sat down again and buried his head in his hands.

Henry Standing, who was sitting next to him, put his hand on his shoulder. "My dear chap, I am so sorry. I think I can say for all of us here, how sorry we are. As far as I am concerned, your religion, or rather the religion you were born into, should have no bearing on your qualification as a member or even the president of the club. You have been a brilliant president for so many years, and everybody knows it. We owe you a lot, and maybe now the time has come to show our mettle, to shake up some of our old rules and regulations. Perhaps it is time that the Evergreen Club entered the 21st century."

"Hear, hear!" came loud and clear the voice of Osbert Harvey. Frederick Brownlow smiled.

"I can see a time in the future, maybe ten years, maybe twenty years, when everyone will be vetted in the same way and admitted on merit," Harry Standing continued.

Gonzalez looked at Mrs. Miller and said, "This is indeed a very interesting evening, full of new information, but it seems we are still in the dark about the man who committed the crime."

Molly answered swiftly: "Agent Gonzalez, are you so sure our murderer is a man? Any reasonably strong and healthy woman could club an unsuspecting man to death, hit a golf ball and make her get away. What do you think?"

Gonzalez blinked. "You are not saying that one of the ladies here... is under suspicion?"

"I am not a feminist, Agent Gonzalez. I don't insist on equal rights, only on equal opportunities... and it seems to me that a woman might have had the same chance to kill Frank as a man..."

Everybody now paid full attention. The gentlemen's eyes wandered along the table from woman to woman: Sheila, Peggy, Marjorie, Marylou, Birdie, Molly herself, and Lucy. They looked at each other.

"...Even a woman who pretends to be old and a helpless cripple!"

To everybody's utter amazement, Molly, who had gotten out of her chair, grasped Lucy de Silva's crutches and flung them forcefully across the room. She turned to Lucy, who remained frozen in her seat. Her face was suddenly deathly white.

"You don't really need these anymore, do you, Lucy? Or should I say Lily? Because you are not my friend Lucy—you are Lily, the actress, the mother of Gail, pretending to be the older, crippled sister."

There was pandemonium. People jumped up from the table, shrieked, someone collected the crutches. Only the woman they all knew as Lucy de Silva remained calm, as if all this excitement had nothing to do with her. She slowly got up, without any physical discomfort, and poured herself a glass of water.

Gonzalez had instinctively moved towards the door to block her way, in case she made an attempt to escape, but she only looked at him and smiled.

"Don't worry. I won't make a run for it. I'm sure you have some of your men out there. Yes, Molly is right, I did it and I am not sorry. He deserved it. I think we have established the fact that he was not a "nice man". Not only was he a domineering bully, as many of you know, he was also a cad! He ruined not only my life, but that of my daughter and her unborn child. He was a callous, cruel man... but no court would have found him guilty for what he did, so I had to take the law into my own hands. It is done... and frankly, I don't care what happens to me now." With these words she sat down again, looking pale but composed.

Gonzalez turned to Molly and asked: "Will you please tell us what just happened? You, Mrs. Miller, obviously had it all figured out before we assembled here tonight."

After a moment's hesitation Molly answered. "From what I learned, Francis Robertson met Lily's daughter Gail in Mexico, after his wife died. He was much taken with the beautiful young woman and they had a passionate affair. Gail had grown up virtually without a father, and she thought that this wealthy, good-looking older man would fulfill all her longing and need for support, love and security.

"I don't know to what extent Frank was aware of her vulnerability, her occasional dependence on drugs and all that. What we do know is that on his third visit to San Miguel, he broke up with her in a rather insensitive fashion. She made a scene, was hysterical, and that made him even more determined not to have anything to do with her anymore. He left Mexico abruptly. What he didn't know was that by then, she was pregnant with his child. When he left her, she was so distraught that she took refuge in drugs. She drugged herself, drank... and died.

"Her mother Lily was called. When she arrived, she found her child dead, and heard the whole dreadful story. I don't know when she decided to take revenge, probably when she found out that her daughter was carrying a child. She knew about Frank from Gail's letters, his address and his circumstances, even details about his household, so she traveled to Florida, intent on avenging her daughter's death.

"Disguised as a man, it was an easy thing to meet Maurice Dutroix at the races and make inquiries about his boss. It would have been difficult to be admitted to the house, so she made up her mind to kill him on the golf course.

"She transformed herself into her dead older sister. I hadn't seen either of them for so many years that it was easy enough to fool me, at least for a while. Through me, she had access to the club, could observe Frank, and wouldn't arouse suspicion as a poor, crippled, elderly lady. Lily rented a room at the Colony Hotel. She asked expressly for one overlooking the golf course, as the concierge told me when I made inquiries. That she had been given this particular room by default was one of the many lies she told me.

"She saw that her victim left every morning at the same time for the golf course, played his five holes, waved at some stage to Henry and returned home.

"On the morning she had chosen for the murder, she was ready, dressed in the same sort of trousers that he usually wore. From the window of her hotel room she could see what color polo shirt he was wearing. She had stocked up on the type of shirts he liked. She took a similar one from her cupboard and an identical blue baseball cap and carried them with her in a little bag. With her crutches she made her way across the road until she came to a gap in the hedge that separated the fairway from Golfview Road. She hid one of her crutches, pulled the polo shirt, golf gloves and the baseball cap out of her bag, put them on, and walked towards the secluded spot between the 10th and the 13th fairway, that she had earmarked. Her one crutch she carried upside down, to make it look like a walking stick from afar. At 8:15, after he had finished the 10th hole, she met up, as planned, with Frank.

"She called and walked over to him. Then they had, I presume, quite an emotional scene. She told him that she had come to avenge her daughter Gail. Frank dismissed her with a shrug and turned around. At that precise moment Lily swung her crutch, hit Frank on the head with the metal base and he fell, stunned, to the ground. She then pulled one of his iron clubs out of the bag, the sand wedge, a deadly weapon, and hit him again and again until he lay in a pool of blood. He was dead.

"She dropped the club next to the body obscured by the shrubs. She picked up Frank's golf bag and walked back to the place near the fence, where she had hidden the other crutch. She left the second one there as well and made her way to the 13th tee. All this was easy to accomplish in fifteen or twenty minutes. As she had seen Frank do, she waved to Henry, and hit a golf ball, rather too well as we have heard. She walked back to Frank and left his golf bag near his body.

"The deed was done, she was ready to leave. Back at the fence she changed her top, cleaned her bloody crutch with the clothes she had taken off, and stuffed them into her bag. Later she was going to dispose of them. Now she was poor, crippled Lucy again, and ready to join me at the golf pavilion for breakfast."

Everybody was too stunned to say anything. Only Special Agent Gonzalez, looking positively miserable, had questions. "How did you find all that out, Mrs. Miller? When did you first get suspicious?"

"I must confess, quite early on. Yes, I believed her when she claimed to be Lucy. After all, I had not seen her or her sister for almost fifty years, and of course there was a family resemblance. However, while Lucy, the real one I mean, had brown eyes, Lily had blue ones. This is something you can change with contact lenses, as I was told by our excellent optician on Peruvian Avenue. To ascertain that this is what she did, I had to have access to her bedroom and bathroom. Well, with a few white lies I achieved that. When I turned up at her hotel room, unannounced, she had no time to hide the contact lenses in her bathroom, nor the binoculars in her bedroom, that she used to observe Frank on the golf course.

"But my first suspicion was aroused right after the murder. Lucy/Lily claimed to have walked straight from the Colony Hotel to the golf pavilion, but her shoes were wet. She would normally have just walked on pavement along Golfview Road, so how could her shoes be all wet, unless she had walked through grass... on the golf course?

"I was still not certain of her guilt. So I tried to trap her. I took her to the Church Mouse. Obediently, she put on various clothes in the fitting room. I sat outside and watched her. The fitting room doors, as you all will know, are open on the top and bottom, so you can see tall people's heads and everybody's lower legs and feet. Well, Lucy, who thought she was safe in the fitting room, moved around in there quite comfortably without crutches, unaware that I could see that. After that, I had no more doubts that she was not crippled. So who could she be, if she was not my friend Lucy? She had to be Lily. Lily, incidentally, was a good athlete in her youth. I didn't know that she played golf, but clearly she is good—perhaps too good—at it."

"Something else gave her away. Lucy and I had been quite interested in physics and chemistry at school. Lily didn't have a clue about these things! She was the artistic one, concentrating on literature and art. So, when Lucy came to my apartment, I engineered an electricity failure. This was easy: I had noticed that there was always a blackout, when I used too many electrical appliances simultaneously. When it happened, she clearly didn't know what to do. The real Lucy would have known how to turn a circuit breaker back on, and what the difference was between 120 and 220 volt electricity.

"What else? Oh yes, Lucy claimed never to have been in Mexico. However, when we were entertained at a party by a small Mexican orchestra, she knew instantly that they are called 'Mariachi'. This was not conclusive, of course, but it confirmed my suspicions. Lucy had to be Lily, and she was the murderer. She had a motive, the opportunity, and the skill, and she had woven a net of deceit around herself to mislead everybody."

Molly paused. She was obviously upset and seemed suddenly tired. "I am sorry, Lily, about what happened to your daughter. I am truly sorry, but I could not let you get away with it. By the way," she turned to the woman who sat with her head bowed next to her, "you gave me a clue, I imagine unintentionally, which I didn't immediately understand. When I asked you about your favorite book, you said 'Hamlet'. Well, if ever there was a story about revenge for a murdered relation, this is it."

Ironically it was Lily, the woman they all knew as Lucy, who extended her hand to Molly, looked at her and said softly: "I am sorry too. You know, I didn't really expect to get away with it, but I had to try. My life without my darling daughter is not worth living anyway. I had to do it, for Gail." With these words she got up and with a nod to Gonzalez, walked to the door.

164

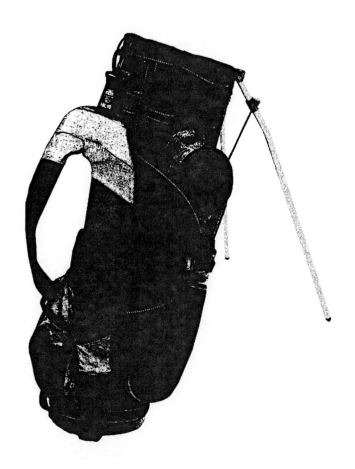

EPILOGUE

It was nine o'clock on a fine May morning in Palm Beach. Under a bright sun beaming down from the eternally blue sky, the happy little island glittered, glowed and sparkled. Molly Miller left the golf pavilion of the Evergreen Club after a good breakfast. In accordance with the season she was dressed in cool, loose-fitting clothes. A blue linen skirt was teamed with a white muslin blouse, short sleeved, printed with small blue flowers. A charming off-white straw hat with a blue ribbon hid her lovely brown hair but protected her face, as did a pair of oversized horn-rimmed sun glasses. She crossed the parking lot, passing the tennis courts, which were all occupied. The early morning hours were the best to play at this time of year. Molly lingered at the enclosure, checking whether she knew any of the players. Indeed, there was Osbert, immaculately turned out and also wearing a straw hat with an incongruously wide rim, considering his athletic pursuit. When he spotted her, he mouthed his favorite greeting: "Kisses! Kisses!" Of his three partners, Molly only recognized her friend Birdie, who made up for her lack of expertise with a stunning white tennis dress. When she looked up, she recognized Molly and waved enthusiastically.

Mrs. Miller waved back and continued on her way to Worth Avenue. She was determined to make this a serious walk rather than a short stroll. The excellent cuisine she was enjoying at the club as well as at home, had rendered the waistband of her skirts and trousers uncomfortably tight. To this end, she had swapped, yet again, her high heels for comfortable sneakers. What a delightful morning, she thought, maybe I could visit the Church Mouse today. Instantly her mind brought up visions and memories of the shocking events that happened barely four weeks before, in which the "Mouse" had played a minor part. Hardly a day had passed, when Molly didn't think back of the events that lead to the discovery of "Lucy" as the murderer.

Their little community had erupted in turmoil, but things had settled back down surprisingly quickly in the intervening weeks. A proper funeral service had taken place for Francis Robertson at Bethesda-by-the Sea after the earlier hasty interment. Special Agent Gonzalez, who had become almost a friend to Molly, had returned to West Palm Beach and to his regular life with the excellent Teresa. He had promised to come and see her whenever he was in the neighborhood. Frederick Brownlow had remained, to everybody's relief, in his position as president of the Evergreen Club. Osbert Harvey continued his inspired leadership of Palm Beach's social life, and at home did his best to placate his increasingly demanding mother.

Molly made her way across Worth Avenue and walked towards her beloved Vias. Unencumbered by traffic and relatively quiet this late in the season, the narrow little lanes wound along picturesque courtyards, beckoning the well-heeled to spend. The shops were, as always, bursting onto the pavement with the glitzy goods Palm Beach shoppers like to buy: antiques (some were even genuine), knickknacks, silk dresses and cashmere in all the colors of the rainbow, dazzling jewelry, fine leatherwork and seductive lingerie.

Having feasted her eyes on the treasures of Via Mizner, Molly now entered Via Parigi. She stopped at the big plate glass window of an art gallery. Inside, a couple, with their backs to her, was looking at a row of oil paintings stacked against the wall. The woman talked, gesticulating, making a point. The young man next to her smiled and nodded his assent. When the woman turned, she recognized Mrs. Miller and waved her in. She rushed forward to open the door and greeted her visitor affectionately.

"Hello you two, you seem to be having a great time." With these words Molly addressed the couple, who were none other than Marylou and Sam.

"We are," agreed Marylou, giving Sam a tender look. "Running a gallery is so much more fun when you have a partner, even if he is a philistine lawyer from New York."

"The legal training may yet be useful when one of your customers discovers that you have sold him a fake or stolen goods," replied Sam with a grin.

"Heaven forbid!" groaned Marylou. She turned to Mrs. Miller and explained: "Sam and I are preparing a new exhibition. Thanks to my new partner's considerable financial clout, we can now champion artists that we really like, even if they are not a guaranteed commercial success. This is so rewarding and something I always wanted to do."

"I'm glad. Does that mean that you are staying in Palm Beach, Sam?" Mrs. Miller wanted to know.

"Well, I'd better. I don't trust my new partner enough yet to leave her alone for any length of time. And she is determined to teach me all I need to know about running a gallery. It looks as if I have gotten myself into a long-term commitment." With this mock complaint the clearly very happy young man turned back to the pictures.

"What about Sheila?" Mrs. Miller wanted to know. "Is she still here? And have you made any decisions about the house?"

"Sheila and Bill went home, one hell of a happy couple. I didn't recognize my sister once she got over the shock of our father's death and had it out with Bill. She looked ten years younger and was behaving like a love-struck teenager. And Bill was a new man, not the unwanted son-in-law who didn't quite make it in business. You know, he really is a very nice guy, and given the right circumstances I am convinced he will succeed with his plans. Even Willie finally came out of his shell and played some golf with me. They all promised to come back and see us regularly, at least twice a year. We decided to sell the house. There are some sad memories in the place and you know how costly it is to maintain such a white elephant. Martin Harris made us a very decent offer for it. He showed us the plans he has for dividing the property, and we like it very much. Sheila and I will both retain an apartment and there will be enough cash left over to keep us happy. And for Martin it's still a good deal. So he and Peggy are happy."

"What about Gil and Morreen?" Mrs. Miller wanted to know.

"Oh, Morreen really enjoyed herself here. She thought the place was like a film set, and the murder like a Hitchcock drama, arranged just for her. Gil was afraid she might never want to leave, but luckily her agent wanted her in New York for auditions, and eventually she flew back, reluctantly. And Gil, well, he is now the proud owner of a remarkable collection of snuff bottles. Sheila and I both agreed that he should have them." Sam looked at Marylou and grinned. "He is still here, slaving over his computer, writing his epic novel. This time he is really serious about it. Apparently, Birdie is determined not to see him until his book is finished. We will keep you posted."

Marylou smiled and added: "We are definitely keeping an eye on those two."

170

"What about the rest of the household?" There was no stopping Molly now.

"Oh, yes, Mrs. Pitts has decided to move to Miami with her son. With the legacy from my father they want to open a restaurant. Not a bad idea! Maurice agreed to stay on for a while longer, till the house is emptied out, but he is planning to return to 'la belle France'. He claims the racing there is far superior, I guess the betting too. I wonder how long his legacy will last! That's about all the news to report about the Robertson household.

"Do you have any news about Lucy, or rather Lily?" Sam wanted to know.

"Well, she is in Miami, in a low-security prison, waiting for her trial. I helped her find an excellent lawyer. I wanted to see her, but so far she refused all visits. She did write to me, however, saying that she might welcome a meeting in a few weeks, when she feels stronger. What she did was of course a dreadful crime, even considering the circumstances. However, if there is anything I can do for her, she only has to ask."

Marylou impulsively hugged the older woman. "You are a dear, Molly, you know... dreaded by criminals all over the world, loved by the whole of Palm Beach."

"And how is Manolita?" Sam cut in. "I heard a rumor that she quit smoking." He loved to pull her leg and could barely keep a straight face.

Molly, lifting an imaginary cigarette in her hand, rose to the occasion. "Ha, isse not true, que pena."

"And you, Molly? Tell us, what are you up to today?" Marylou wanted to know.

"Well, as you can see," she pointed at her sneakers, "I'm prepared for a good, long walk... and after that I have a lunch date."

"This wouldn't by any chance be with a certain gentleman who wears dashing bow ties and drives a fashionable soft-top vintage Chevrolet, would it?" Marylou could not resist the tease.

"It could well be," was Mrs. Miller's coy answer, as she bid the young couple good bye.

About the Author

Dagmar Lowe was born in Germany and studied German and English literature and history of art in Switzerland (lic. phil. University of Zurich). She is a translator of note, a broadcaster for the BBC and writes as a journalist in English and German. Her work has been published in the Evening Standard, Daily Telegraph, Literary Review etc. She lives with her four children in London and on the island of Palm Beach.

This is her first novel, but apparently her "accidental sleuth", Molly Miller, is already involved in a new case.

Lightning Source UK Ltd.
Milton Keynes UK
14 January 2010

148624UK00001B/142/A